ISBN-13: 9798989795123

Cover design by: Art Painter

Library of Congress Control Number: 2018675309

Printed in the United States of America

Dark Fleet

By Daniel Schloss

Character List - Dark Fleet

Jacob Westerly – Federal Special Agent

Cassius Stone - Supervising Special Agent of the FinCEN Unit

Jonathan "Jack" Bennett – Assistant Director of FinCEN Unit

Pyotr "Peter" Stanislavski – Russian Oligarch, Father of Anya

Anya Lenkov (A.K.A. Stanislavski) – Daughter of Peter Stanislavski, and Jacob's ex-wife

Sergey Valenki - Head of Security for Peter Stanislavski

Arminio Tommaso – Waiter who was given a camera after the explosion.

The Praetorian – The unknown person feeding info to Peter and Anya

Robby Powell - The 10-year-old nemesis of Cassius Stone

Olivia Hawthorne – MI6 Agent

Hamish Crowe – MI6 Agent

Nabil Massoudo – Cameraman working for Peter and Anya, being blackmailed by the Kremlin

Maximilian "Max" Schmidt – Police Detective, Hamburg Police

Johann "John" von Steinhardt – INTERPOL agent

Lukas "Luke" Müller – Male Prostitute

Don Chamberlin – California Deputy Attorney General

Robert Miller – Deputy Attorney General, California Department of Justice

Santino Cruz – Filipino Assassin working for the CIA, who is trying to learn more about Nabil

Alessandro Bianchi, Agente di Polizia di Interpol, assigned to Forte del Marmi, Italy

Uncle Dmitri Stanislavski, Anya's Uncle, Peter's brother. Owner of the Villa

Federal Law Enforcement Training Center (FLETC) in Glynco, Georgia

Maxim Volkov – Wealthy Oligarch who had the Mussolini letter in Italy.

Senior Airman Donna Walters – Loadmaster on C-130 out of Ramstein AFB, Germany.

Captain Bill Hickock, pilot of the C-130 transporting Stone to the States.

Jay Lim, Driver and Fixer, used in Seoul, South Korea

Tom – intelligence handler to Nabil in Afghanistan

Isabella – A Young Cuban girl who lived with Nabil on a sailboat

Robert – Watched ships explode.

Tola – Jacobs Maine Coon cat from his days in San Francisco

Chuck Hoover, Master Sergeant – Boyfriend of Natalia

Natalia – Foreign Agent handling Master Sergeant Chuck Hoover

Lucy Hoover – Stateside wife of Master Sergeant Chuck Hoover, stationed in Germany.

Tonya – Jacob and Lisa's friend from San Francisco, who notified Jacob of Lisa's death.

CHAPTER 1 (Killing Peter)

The man stared at himself in the large gold-framed shower mirror, his face covered in shaving cream. As he thought this would be his last pull of shaving foam from his chin, he winced in pain and wiped the blood away with a tissue. But as he did, he noticed something strange. The blood was not red, but black. Not thick and sticky, but watery. He squinted with concern, having seen nothing like this before. Touching the wound with his finger, his skin felt cold and clammy. And was starting to itch. The man quickly finished shaving and got out of the shower. Should he call his personal assistant or the army of bodyguards just outside the door? He went to the kitchen and got a glass of water. Feeling lightheaded, he sat down at the table and put his head in his hands, not knowing what was wrong with him, he was starting to get concerned. His eyes closed as he tried to focus his mind on the symptoms. He thought about his daughter, who was lost somewhere in the United States and unreachable. But the darkness was closing in. He felt himself slipping away as everything went black.

The man's body was limp as they loaded him into the German Rettungswagen. His eyes were closed, and his breathing was shallow. The paramedics worked frantically to stabilize him, but his symptoms showed he was in terrible shape. As the ambulance sped through the streets, the man periodically woke up. He would open his eyes briefly, look around in confusion, and then close them again. He was not aware of what was happening to him.

"Anya, Anya," he yelled before lapsing back into a semi-unconscious state.

The paramedic glanced at the name on his clipboard, which explained the presence of a sizable group of bodyguards. Two of them remained seated next to him, carefully observing the attending paramedic's actions. Peter Stanislavski, the wealthiest Russian oligarch, resided outside of Moscow, away from his home. The paramedics did their best to keep Peter calm, but he was agitated, moaning and mumbling incoherently.

Upon the ambulance's arrival at Martin Luther Hospital in Berlin, Peter was swiftly transported into the emergency room. Inside, the medical staff operated with remarkable efficiency, executing tasks such as drawing blood, establishing intravenous lines, and promptly informing the laboratory of the situation at hand. Hospital security quickly secured the entire hospital floor in anticipation of the man's arrival, while his bodyguards ensured a clear path for his passage. Given the critical nature of his condition, the doctors harbored uncertainty regarding his chances of survival. Nevertheless, they spared no effort in their endeavors to save his life.

The man's initial hours progressed slowly but steadily. Although the doctors suspected he had an infection with polonium-210, they hesitated to disclose this information to him. Nevertheless, they reassured him that every possible measure was being taken to aid his recovery, yet they could not guarantee a complete restoration of his health.

Feeling disoriented and bewildered, Peter was at a loss as how he had contracted the infection and what lay ahead for him. Suddenly, a flashback of the morning's events rushed back to his memory—the moment when he accidentally nicked himself while shaving, causing blood to flow.

"Sergey, clear the room. I must speak with you," he demanded in a pronounced Russian accent, his tone carrying a sense of urgency.

His guards promptly escorted the medical staff out of the room, leaving Peter alone with Sergey, his trusted head of security, in an empty chamber. Sergey had remained steadfastly by Peter's side ever since they had discovered him following an assassination attempt on Peter's life. Sergey's quick thinking and remarkable physical conditioning saved Peter from an assassin's blade. A scar etched across Sergey's right cheek served as a constant reminder of that pivotal moment—a testament to the intervention of a stranger, a trained FSB Agent, who took it upon himself to thwart the man hell-bent on killing Peter Stanislavski. Peter owed Sergey a debt he would never forget.

"The razor. Locate it and have it tested. We need to determine how someone gained access to an item that should have been beyond reach."

Peter's coughing fit became uncontrollable, prompting the medical staff to swiftly respond, despite their initial reluctance to bypass the imposing sentry. Hurrying to aid their patient, Peter managed to speak, albeit with incredible difficulty.

"I presume, doctor, that I was poisoned. Any thoughts on what it might have been?" he managed to utter; his voice barely audible.

The German doctor hesitated to reveal his suspicions, apprehensive that divulging such information could reach the ears of the assassin, potentially endangering the doctor's safety simply for possessing this knowledge.

"At this juncture, we are unable to ascertain with certainty. Your symptoms bear resemblance to other cases of poisonings we have encountered, and they appear to be originating from a singular source."

"Source? What source? Tell me who is responsible for this. What was used? Doctor, you know, and I demand you give me the information!" Peter nearly shouted; his frustration evident. However, before the doctor could respond, Peter's eyes rolled back in his head, and he collapsed onto the bed. The monitor adjacent to him detected electrical signals from his heart, which emitted a piercing, loud sound, indicating that his heart had ceased to beat.

Chaos ensued in the room as organized training took hold. Peter's bed was swiftly adjusted into a supine position, with his upper clothing opened to provide access to his chest. The noise emanating from the nearby machine grew louder while a doctor prepared the defibrillator pads coated in gel.

"Clear!" the doctor shouted, alerting the other medical staff of the imminent 500-volt shock that would be administered to Peter's body. As the doctor pressed the buttons on the hand pads, Peter's torso arched in response, only to forcefully collapse back onto the bed. The monitor displayed a single flat line, emitting the same monotonous tone.

"750," he repeated to the technician operating the machine.

A few seconds elapsed as the machine gathered strength. This time, the shock of electricity surged through Peter's body, causing his upper body to arch almost entirely off the bed. All eyes shifted to the monitor, where a faint heartbeat registered. Gradually, his heartbeat intensified, instilling confidence in everyone present that this would not be Peter Stanislavski's final day on Earth.

Sergey observed the scene from the side of the room. He then turned swiftly and departed, whispering a message into the ear of the bodyguard assigned to the room. It was crucial to locate the razor before anyone could dispose of the evidence. Sergey understood that the type of poison involved would provide vital information regarding the responsible party even though they all harbored suspicions.

The camera quietly clicked as the man wearing a ball cap with a Boston Red Sox emblem shot photos of the large man in a dark suit, wearing an earbud as he left the hospital. Sergey was a man on a mission, and his trained lifestyle would have normally let him see the man on the other side of the street following his every move with the camera. But today, Sergey was laser-focused on one thing: get the razor. The electronic FOB on his key chain signaled once that he was within unlocking distance of the car. He paused and waited. His heart rate increased, knowing that something was not right. Slowly, he raised the FOB and pushed the unlock button. The door locks opened. His body relaxed as he moved forward and entered the Mercedes; his mission was back on track.

The man with the camera relaxed; he had gotten what he had come for. As he lifted his cup of coffee, the explosion's impact knocked him off his seat. Car alarms blared, and his ears were ringing. The garden barrier separating him from the café and the street provided concealment but not cover. Blood ran from his ear as he grabbed the camera and stumbled to stand. The front of the hospital was ablaze with the remanence of diesel that had ignited as it flew from the parked car. A shell of the car was left where, moments ago, a young, well-dressed Russian had pushed the button to start the engine. His chard-burning figure was slumped back against the seat.

"Sir, are you all right?" the waiter asked the man on the floor, who was attempting to stand.

"Yes, yes, I'm fine," as the man collapsed. The waiter was unable to hold the weight of his falling body.

"What is your name?" the bleeding man asked, grabbing the waiter's shirt.

"Arminio," he said in the ear that was not bleeding.

"Arminio, give this to the Praetorian," the man said in a near catatonic state as he handed the waiter the broken camera. "The Praetorian," the man yelled louder.

Arminio took the camera, hiding it under his white coat, blackened with soot and blood. Leaving the unconscious man on the ground, he placed the camera in his bag located in the backroom. He returned to give more aid to the customer, only to find him gone.

Arminio thought to himself as he winced from the heat of the flames across the street; who was the Praetorian? How would I find him, or would he find me?

CHAPTER 2 (First day on the job)

"It was here last night!" his voice on the phone sounded confused.

"How do you lose a ten-thousand-ton ship?" Agent Stone asked, annoyance evident in his voice.

"You don't, obviously. Someone stole it and killed my officer," the male voice nearly yelled, his broken English betraying his attempt to avoid sounding like an idiot. "Our Duty Officer left for a minute, and when he returned, the ship was gone, and the Dock Officer was lying in a pool of his blood."

"Take a photo of your man's face and send the damn thing to my cell phone, along with his name," Stone insisted. Moments later, his cell phone buzzed, and a photo of the dead Dock Officer had been received.

"Ok, got it. An agent from our office will be there shortly. I expect you to cooperate fully. Understood?"

"We did nothing wrong here. We did our jobs," the voice said, justifying his existence.

Stone's long-distance phone call yielded more unanswered questions than he anticipated. Frustrated, he slammed the phone down with such force that it fractured near his coffee cup, adorned with the FinCEN (Financial Crimes Enforcement Network) logo. Supervising Treasury Agent Cassius Stone stared at the wall, overcome with disbelief.

His daily routine remained unchanged as he arrived at work promptly at 7:00 am. Being an early riser, Stone indulged in a customary espresso accompanied by a lightly toasted piece of rye bread before leaving home. This morning ritual had persisted for over fifteen years, spanning nearly three decades of his career. However, the stress of the situation was taking its toll as his stomach began to burn—a sign of the ulcer that his doctor had diagnosed. The lack of answers from untrained police officers only added to his frustration.

Stone stood stationary, looking out the tall glass windows making up his office. Photos on the walls were few but reflected a career spent as a Federal Agent.

Agent Jacob Westerly walked into the sea of desks, making up the FinCEN Unit, sitting at a desk that was absent of personal items.

"Agent Westerly, not your desk!" Stone exclaimed, his voice rising in volume. He pointed towards a corner where a gray metal desk accompanied by a leaning chair appeared neglected. "That one's yours. Get settled, then come see me." With that, Stone turned and made his way into his office.

On his first day, Jacob experienced a sense of confusion. In his previous job at Citation Software, the boss had warmly received him and introduced him to everyone as a highly valued addition that the company had eagerly awaited. People shook his hand, engaged in casual conversations, and extended warm welcomes wherever he went, embracing him as a part of the team. Things were different here.

The few agents sitting at their desks in FinCEN stole only glances in Jacob's direction as he made his way to Stone's glass-walled office—perhaps out of curiosity about the recruit or to size him up and assess how long he would last. Stone gestured towards the empty chair in his office, silently urging Jacob to sit. However, Jacob remained standing.

"Sit when you can. Things get hectic around here real fast, and you'll appreciate the chance to rest your feet," Stone advised as he settled into his chair, with Jacob following suit. "Have you finished moving into your new place?"

"Well, if you consider living out of unmarked brown boxes as being moved in," Jacob replied.

"Good. So, you're done with academy training. You have a shiny new badge and title. I hope your gun is clean and on your belt! Don't be like the others down there," Stone said, pointing towards the gradually filling gray desks. "Your gun won't do you any good in your desk. You and I will be going places and stirring up trouble, and I want to make sure you have my back just as I have yours."

Jacob felt a surge of excitement coursing through him. He had made a complete 180-degree turn from his previous job, where he was comfortable, stationed at a desk in the warm confines of California's Bay Area. This was the big leagues now—a realm that demanded responsibility and clear thinking. FinCEN belonged to an elite group of highly skilled men and women, each carefully selected for their unique abilities.

Stone sat, his gaze fixed on Jacob, his forehead wrinkling and his lips curling as he carefully pondered his words. He was mindful of the message he conveyed to the new agent, striving to strike the right balance.

"When people take something from me, it pisses me off," Stone declared, his voice filled with conviction. "When I was eight years old, I had a ritual with my father. Every evening before dinner, I would place my baseball mitt on the porch, and he would oil it before leaving for work the next morning. That smell of oiled leather still brings back memories of my dad. But one day, I went outside to get my mitt, and it was gone. I felt empty, and my stomach ached. Two days later, I saw my mitt on the hand of Robby Powell, a ten-year-old thug from my neighborhood. Robby was a bully, always taking whatever he wanted. Anger built up inside me—the kind that no ten-year-old should ever have to experience."

Jacob, trying not to appear clueless, asked, "Did you get your mitt back?"

"I went downstairs into the basement and took the 4-iron from my dad's golf bag," Stone continued a determined expression on his face. "As I walked out the back door, there was my dad. He understood exactly what I was feeling. He told me to go talk with Robbie, to negotiate without resorting to violence. And once I got my mitt back, before I turned to leave, he wanted me to shake Robby's hand. That was the day I learned the importance of walking softly but carrying a big stick."

"And did Robby go along with the plan?" Jacob inquired; curiosity was evident in his voice.

Stone replied, a hint of a smile playing on his lips, "He handed me the mitt, and I shook his hand. Maybe it was the sight of the 4-iron in my hand or the determination in my eyes. I leaned over and whispered in his ear, 'If you ever take anything from me again, I will crush your head like a bug.' I smiled and turned away. My dad witnessed me shaking Robby's hand and returning with the mitt, without resorting to the use of his golf club. Sometimes, things are better left unexplained."

Jacob sat there, contemplating the story and wrestling with Stone's message. "Do I trust this guy?" he wondered, finding it surprising to have such thoughts on his first day of work. But Stone had proven himself in past situations with Jacob, demonstrating that he could be trusted.

"Someone is taking things from us, the Treasury Department," Stone revealed with a grave tone. "We seize assets from Russian oligarchs, and within days, they vanish. Some cases involve murders. The pattern is consistent across all the thefts; regardless of location, the MO is the same."

Jacob's mind flashed back to his time at the Federal Law Enforcement Training Center (FLETC) in Glynco, Georgia, where he had learned the meaning of "MO" or "Modus operandi" for criminal behavior. It was a particular method of operation, a term he had heard on TV but truly grasped during his training.

Stone handed him a piece of paper bearing the logos of the Department of Justice and FinCEN. Stamped diagonally across the page was the word "CONFIDENTIAL."

Jacob was left stunned as he read the list of high-value items stolen after being seized in various locations worldwide. The implications were challenging to comprehend.

"A 180-foot super yacht?" Jacob exclaimed; his voice filled with astonishment. "Boss, I used to own one of these. It's not like you can simply turn the ignition switch, put it in drive, and sail off. It requires a well-trained team and a meticulously planned operation."

His thoughts wandered to Anastasia's Dream, a chapter of his life that had come to an end when he sold the ship. He reminisced about the 290-foot vessel he had owned, which had become his possession after a Russian oligarch's fraudulent attempt to hack the auction site. This illicit act enabled Jacob to acquire the ship, but it also led to an assassination attempt orchestrated by the oligarch's daughter. Jacob's decision to sell the ship resulted in a substantial windfall of millions of dollars. He wisely stored the funds in offshore accounts to safeguard his wealth from envious Russian hackers.

"An Airbus A321, 100 kilograms of gold bars, priceless rare paintings, ancient Roman antiquities, and a collection of valuable first edition books. How can you fly off with a full-sized jet and smuggle all these items without anyone noticing?" Jacob questioned, his disbelief evident in his voice.

"Now you're starting to grasp the magnitude of this situation," Stone replied, his tone grave. "The FBI and CIA have been trying to assist, but they've been running in circles. I may have some answers. Go home and pack your bags, Jacob. We're heading to London in two hours. I'll explain everything during our flight."

CHAPTER 3 (London)

Arminio stood on the bustling street corner two minutes early, his heart pounding excitedly. Downtown Hamburg is a vibrant metropolis of activity, bustling with life and energy. Every street corner beckoned with a diverse array of eateries, enticing the senses with the aromas of international cuisines wafting through the air. From charming cafes serving freshly brewed coffee and warm pastries to upscale restaurants offering gastronomic delights, the culinary scene catered to every palate. He had just pulled off a major score—the 35 mm digital DSLR camera securely held in his right hand. Concealed behind sunglasses, he scanned the crowd, searching for his contact with the key to his payoff.

"Arminio! Come va, fratello?" a voice called out in Italian.
Turning his back to the street, Arminio broke into a smile as his contact approached. The momentary distraction was all it took. Unbeknownst to Arminio, a black sprinter van glided silently behind him, its sliding door opening without a sound.

A split second later, a Taser pressed against Arminio's neck, delivering a sharp sting. Fifty thousand volts coursed through his body, rendering him limp. The camera slipped from his grasp and was snatched away by the assailant. Before his body hit the ground, two burly men, acting in perfect synchrony, swooped in, grabbing Arminio under his armpits, effortlessly lifting him, and swiftly depositing him into the waiting van. In less than 20 seconds, it was all over. The van smoothly pulled away from the scene, leaving the witnesses to choose noninvolvement as they turned and walked on, pretending not to have seen anything.

◆ ◆ ◆

Bypassing TSA with a swift flash of their government agency badges, Jacob and Stone effortlessly skipped the long lines, shedding the hassle of removing their shoes and enduring the cumbersome security measures that falsely reassured people of their safety when flying. Their credentials granted them expedited access, sparing the two agents valuable time and allowing them to proceed directly to the departure gates.

Thirty thousand feet above the vast expanse of the Atlantic Ocean, Stone, sitting beside Jacob, pulled out his tablet. Activating a cutting-edge security protocol, he engaged a sophisticated encryption mechanism that shielded their communications from prying eyes. The state-of-the-art technology ensured that no electronic devices within their vicinity could copy or intercept the encrypted messages, safeguarding the sensitive information they possessed.

"MI6 contacted our agency with alarming information regarding an Italian individual who attempted to sell them a camera. This device supposedly held photographs of individuals and objects that the photographer deemed highly valuable. Intriguingly, an undercover MI6 Agent, posing as a local criminal, arranged a meeting with the Italian to purchase the camera. However, an unsettling pattern emerged: each time a photo was displayed, it inexplicably turned pitch black after a mere second. This brief glimpse was sufficient for the MI6 Agent to discern that valuable assets obtained during our country's raids and those conducted in other nations that were mysteriously missing had been photographed."

"We're they able to identify the Italian?"

"The agent agreed to pay the man his price but delayed, saying he needed time to gather the cash. When the new meeting occurred, a group of agents snatched the man, or as we call it, a 'pull aside' and now have him hidden away in London."

"Where did they grab him? I'm sorry, 'pull him aside'?"

"On a street corner in Hamburg, Germany. We need to go talk with him and get some answers."

"Why are we going to London if he was snatched…pulled aside, in Germany? Aren't the German Police dealing with this?"

"MI6 felt the police might have been compromised, so the Italian was flown out of Germany on a private jet. To make sure it was kept quiet."

The look of Heathrow Airport took Jacob aback. It was huge, clean, and bright. Hundreds of travelers moved about at a choreographed speed. On the flight over, Cassias broke the ice and suggested he call him Cas when out of the ear range of others. Jacob felt more like Cas was now a partner instead of a supervisor, but he always remembered where he stood when it came to orders.

As they neared the waiting area to retrieve their luggage, an older gentleman dressed in a finely tailored three-piece suit approached. Stone caught sight of the man and slowed his pace, while Jacob, unaware of Stone's pause, continued ahead, unknowingly leaving Stone alone.

"Agent Stone?" the man inquired, his voice carrying a distinct Scottish accent. "I'm Hamish Crowe from MI6," he announced, displaying an ID card bearing his younger photograph and the prominently displayed letters "MI6" in vibrant green.

"Special Agent Cassius Stone," Stone introduced himself, extending his hand for a handshake. "And that's Special Agent Jacob Westerly," he added, pointing towards the young and bewildered man who was scanning the area for Stone. With a quick wave and an apologetic expression, he quickly made his way back, attempting not to bump into people while flowing against the tide of travelers.

"I'm sorry, Jacob Wester…Special Agent Jacob Westerly, from America…United States," shaking the man's hand. Stone watched the new kid, shaking hands while balancing his carry-on in the other.

"I'm your contact while in the U.K. Please come this way. Your bags have already been removed from the aircraft and will be in my car shortly," Crowe instructed the agents.

The trio of men approached an inconspicuous, unmarked side door along the hallway. Crowe swiftly produced a white card and pressed it against the digital lock, causing the door to unlatch with a soft click. Crossing the threshold, they found themselves in an empty hallway, only to be joined by a fourth man who was noticeably younger than Crowe and possessed an athlete's physique. Without any formal introduction, the newcomer positioned himself slightly behind the others, matching their brisk pace as they traversed a series of interconnecting corridors. Feeling uneasy, Jacob continually cast furtive glances over his shoulder at the man trailing them, occasionally offering a forced smile to alleviate the tension. However, the man's countenance remained emotionless, fixated on the path ahead.

As they stepped through the doorway labeled "C06," Jacob was greeted by a refreshing breeze, accompanied by the subtle scent of rain. The bustling walkway lay before them, brimming with activity. The man who had been tailing them retrieved a key fob from his pocket, triggering a response from the sleek black Audi A6 as its doors unlocked remotely. Crowe courteously opened the rear passenger door for Stone while the unnamed agent slid into the driver's seat. Observing the unfolding scene, Jacob deduced that his place was in the front passenger seat, next to the stoic and taciturn driver. With everyone settled in their respective positions, the car sprang to life, merging seamlessly into the traffic flow, occasionally cutting off other vehicles. The blaring of horns served as mere background noise to the occupants, except for the youngest U.S. agent, whose grip on the door and center console grew increasingly tense, knuckles turning white.

"Do you still have the Italian man in custody?" Stone asked.

"He awaits your interview after we brief you on some unusual things we discovered. We canceled your reservations at the hotel you selected and rebooked you into an apartment controlled by our office. It is secure of listening devices and has specially designed windows to prevent exterior audio infiltration. All staff have been fully vetted. I think you will find it to your liking."

"Thank you. I look forward to seeing it." As the vehicle raced toward downtown London.

As they rounded the corner onto the A202 bridge, the iconic sight of the Vauxhall Cross SIS Building came into view. Known to the locals as the MI6 building, it stood tall and imposing, housing the Secret Intelligence Service. Its twelve floors soared into the sky, adorned with a distinctive green roof that contrasted against the grey concrete walls. Perched on the banks of the river Thames along the Albert Embankment, it commanded an imposing presence. The structure resembled a fortress, fortified with towering green metal fences that reached for the heavens, adorned with bent, menacing spikes designed to deter anyone contemplating scaling its formidable walls. Jacob's gaze fell upon this bastion of concrete and metal, and he couldn't help but appreciate the English expertise in constructing impenetrable fortifications. It was a testament to their centuries-old legacy in castle-making, ensuring that secrets remained securely guarded within its impressive confines.

The Audi smoothly passed through an unmarked gate, where only a simple blue "IN" sign marked its entrance. There were no visible signs or indications on the building's exterior to reveal its purpose to passersby, whether they were driving, walking, or cycling. The imposing black iron gate swiftly closed behind them, guarded by attentive security personnel who diligently monitored the entrance, ensuring no unauthorized individuals entered. Descending a steep ramp, the car found its place several floors below the surface of the building, where it came to a stop.

"Your bags will be moved to an apartment across the street, when we finish you will be directed to the location. We have an underground tunnel that goes directly to a floor that MI6 maintains for guests and dignitaries." It speaks, Jacob thought as he watched the driver explain.

The elevator stopped on the 6th floor. Exterior light filled the floor as the door opened. To the left of the elevator a pigeonhole box on the wall with keys inserted in unused plexiglass boxes.

"Your phones please." Hamish removed his cellular phone, locked it in a box, and removed the key. Cassius and Jacob did the same.

Following Hamish down the hallway, they arrived at a sturdy door. Stepping inside, they found themselves in a sparsely furnished room, with only a desk and a monitor occupying the space. On the screen sat a solitary figure dressed in an orange jumpsuit and sporting a well-tanned complexion. His left leg was slightly bouncing. An obvious sign that he was nervous and outside his element. Stone observed an ashtray on the desk, although there were no signs of any smoking materials. Directly in front of the man, there sat a small paper cup. The man glanced around the room, his gaze on the camera above. His expression conveyed concern and confusion, evident from his deep breaths and furrowed brow.

"I'd like to speak with the man if you don't have any objections," Stone asked.

"Yes, sir, we suspected as much. However, allow me to update you on our findings first," Hamish replied. Opening the lower drawer, he retrieved a sizable plastic box equipped with a digital biometric finger pad. With a firm press of his finger against the pad, a satisfying snap was heard, activating a small green LED light that illuminated the box.

Carefully lifting the plastic lid, Hamish revealed a 35mm DSLR camera adorned with a black strap, placing it delicately on the table. The camera, a Zenitar-M manufactured in Russia, bore traces of fingerprint powder on its lens. Adjacent to the camera, an evidence envelope contained a digital SD card.

"This is the camera Arminio Tommaso attempted to sell to us, or rather, to our Agent in Germany," Hamish explained. "We fingerprinted the camera, but unfortunately, the prints were compromised due to constant handling. Only Arminio's prints remained discernible."

"What about DNA?" Jacob asked.

Initially, there was nothing significant. The camera had passed through numerous hands, as Arminio claimed to have purchased it from a street vendor," Hamish relayed. He flipped the camera over, revealing the bottom safety latch on the White Wave brand shoulder strap. "However, our technicians struck gold. Right here," he pointed to the screw-in strap hinge, "the previous owner must have accidentally cut themselves while closing it, leaving behind a small sample of skin cells. These cells are recent and fresh, not matching Arminio's DNA. Our experts are confident this DNA belongs to the individual who last handled the camera before Arminio acquired it."

"We can run it through our database for a match," Jacob said with a feeling of excitement as he started to see the pieces of the puzzle come together.

"I don't want you to think you made a trip across the pond for nothing, but we did that and got a hit." Hamish gave a cocky look as if his intel was from superior work.

"And I suppose we need to ask politely for you to tell us?" Stone said sarcastically

"Nabil Massoudo is a 30-year-old Moroccan who has been living in Germany for the past five years. He does odd jobs and can be a muscle for crime bosses who want info, one of which is intelligence gathering for the SVR, the Foreign Intelligence Service of the Russian Federation."

"Have you mentioned this name to Arminio?" Stone asked with concern.

"No, we just reviewed basics, his identity, address, and movements for the past five years," Hamish said while reviewing a written report.

"He has to wonder why you had him snatched off the streets in Hamburg."

"We informed him that it was the idea of the German Bundesnachrichtendienst, the BND. They suspected him of being a bank robber, and his name had an Interpol red flag attached to it," Hamish explained. "However, we intended to discuss something unrelated. Unfortunately, he remains unaware of the true purpose." Hamish reached over and picked up the SD card enclosed in the envelope.

"This is where it becomes intriguing. The SD card contains a vast collection of photos, diagrams, and emails. However, whenever we attempt to open any of them, the photos display for a mere fraction of a second before abruptly closing, rendering them inaccessible. If we make more than two repeated attempts to open any item, the card becomes corrupt, and nothing can be accessed after that. Furthermore, some files require a specific encryption key, and any incorrect input leads to corruption. Although we have created numerous copies to safeguard the original card, an encryption key seems necessary to unlock its contents—a key that our technical experts have yet to decipher."

"Do you know where Massoudo was living? An address?" asked Stone.

"Yes, he was just outside downtown Hamburg in a nice apartment in the Speicherstadt neighborhood. Someone was financially supplementing him."

Stone glanced at Jacob and said, "Let's have a conversation with this guy," pointing to Arminio seated behind the one-way mirror. After both agents secured their duty weapons, backup guns, and knives in a secure box, provided by their guest, they followed Hamish out of the room and stood by an adjacent door. Before opening it, Stone paused, looking towards Jacob.

"This will be our first interview together. Just observe. Pay attention to his body language and refrain from speaking," Stone said. Jacob nodded in agreement.

They entered the room while Hamish stepped back to observe from an adjacent chamber. Jacob's mind wandered back to a previous encounter when Stone had interviewed him—a significant event that had brought their paths together. Reflecting on his own nervousness during that time, Jacob contemplated Arminio's current state. However, the roles had reversed now, with Jacob sitting on the opposite side of the table. Emulating Stone's approach during their initial meeting, Jacob averted his gaze from Arminio. With deliberate intent, Stone strategically positioned his notebook in front of him and neatly placed his pen beside it, creating an atmosphere of heightened suspense. Gradually raising his eyes, Stone maintained silence, yet his gaze locked onto Arminio's, conveying a message without uttering a word.

"Don't speak. We know everything you did." Pausing and looking down at his notes.

"What?" Arminio started to say. Still looking down, Stone lifted his right hand as if ordering a car to stop advancing. Arminio sat quietly.

"You were responsible for the explosion at the hospital, which killed the man in the car, and countless other crimes. Looks like you have a pretty substantial criminal past. Nothing large but annoying to the courts. Arminio let me put it in another context you might better understand. Do you own a cat or a dog?" Stone asked.

Arminio looked confused and then in a low tone replied, "A dog,"

"Let's say that dog of yours keeps pissing on your couch while you're away. No matter what you do, it keeps pissing on your couch. At first, you try to train it. When that fails, you get a bit more forceful, placing it in the backyard for a while to show how annoyed you are. But then one day, just when you think the dog gets the message, you come home and there it is again. That odor, the scent of dog piss again on your couch. Now you're angry; nothing you've done has taught that ungrateful beast a lesson. So, you take it to the dog pound and get rid of it. Now it's someone else's problem. Well, Arminio, every time you show up in front of the Judge, it's like you're pissing on his couch. And eventually, he's going to get tired of seeing you and will just stuff you away somewhere, so he is rid of you," Stone, now standing, partially leaning over the table, arms supporting his body as he hovered over the man whose eyes were large and round.

The room was silent, and you could almost hear Arminio's heart beating.

"Well, I'm going to make sure the Judge knows we have a place you can go that will never allow you to piss on the Judge's couch. Do you know what a black site is?"

In 2006, the knowledge of black sites permeated television broadcasts and cell phone feeds, making it a widely known topic. Then, in 2021, the purpose of these clandestine facilities was revealed through news reports. These sites were designed to isolate individuals, suspected of terrorism from society, subjecting them to interrogation and, in some cases, torture. Stripped of any legal protections, these individuals found themselves without recourse, while governments remained tight-lipped, refusing to acknowledge their existence. Ultimately, they vanished into thin air, leaving no trace of their whereabouts.

Arminio was visibly shaken. His armpits were sweating, and the orange jumpsuit was drenched, unlike moments before when the two Federal Agents had walked into the room. Fearing he would be in trouble by breaking the silence placed upon him by the agent, he sat shaking his head in disbelief.

"Do you have children, Arminio?" Stone asked. Still not daring to speak, he shook his head in affirmation. Stone sighed and tilted his head as if evaluating the man in front of him.

"I know you have an explanation. I want to hear it from you." Stone said.

"I know nothing about the explosion," he said slowly, emphasizing each word as if he wanted Stone to grasp their significance. "I was attending to a customer on the terrace when the car suddenly detonated. The blast knocked both of us to the ground. I had no idea of what had just occurred." Arminio hoped that Stone had comprehended his explanation despite his pronounced accent.

"You were taking pictures from the restaurant. Did you hope to get a photo of the explosion? Proof to your handlers that your mission was accomplished?"

"No," he said, confused. "I was not taking the pictures; my customer was, the man I helped up after the bomb went off," Arminio tried to correct the facts.

"So, you're telling me that the other guy was the one taking the photos, and you ended up selling the camera. Is that how you explain it, Arminio?" Stone's voice slightly rose, expressing his annoyance at being deceived. "Did this guy just approach you and say, 'Hey, Mr. Waiter, want to see some really cool photos?' Oh, and by the way, would you mind holding onto the camera? Is that what you're trying to tell me?"

"Okay, I admit it. I did try to sell the camera. I'm just a common thief, but I'm not involved in bombings!" Arminio's voice trembled with panic as he confessed. "The man handed me the camera and kept insisting, 'Make sure the Praetorian gets this,' as he repeatedly shoved the camera into my hands."

"The Praetorian? Like in Praetorian Guard?"

"Yes, yes, the Praetorian!" Arminio dropped his arms like a man who had just confessed to every crime he had ever committed and was now absolved.

"Who was he? What was his name, Arminio?"

"I have no idea. I went to the back room and put the camera in my bag. When I returned, he was gone. I never saw him again. You have to believe me. You have to!"

Stone shut his notepad and stood up, walking toward the door; Jacob followed. Arminio turned and watched, while still yelling.

"Please don't put me in a black site, please. I will never piss on the Judge's couch again!" his voice was cut short by the slamming of the door behind Stone and Jacob. Hamish came out of the interview room where he had been monitoring the interrogation.

"Interesting way to conduct an interview. In less than 5 minutes, you found a possible puppet master behind this. But who is the Praetorian?" Hamish questioned.

"I don't know. Can you show us to our accommodations and get me a copy of the SD card? One that your techs have not tried to open."

"Already done." Handing Stone, a small plastic box containing three cards. "All three are identical, just in case you erase the first two."

"Good thinking," Stone said, placing the cards in his coat pocket.

The agents were handed the boxes containing their weapons and collected their belongings.

"Right this way, gentlemen. Pissing on the Judge's couch? Interesting analogy, if you don't mind, I might use that one in the future,"

Hamish led the group down the hallway to the elevator. Jacob had imagined the inside of MI6 being guarded by machine gun-toting personnel, closely monitoring their every move. He couldn't help but feel disappointed. The interior of MI6 resembled an ordinary stockbroker's office in D.C. If he hadn't known they were in a super spy facility, he would have never guessed.

CHAPTER 4 (Sea Shanties)

The tunnel leading across the street to their apartment facility was adorned with posters, giving it the appearance of an entrance to a subway station. Stone's attention was caught by a poster depicting several men dressed in old seafarer clothes sitting on whiskey barrels at the end of a dock. The accompanying announcement below the image advertised, "London Sea Shanty Collective, one night only." Stone slowed his pace to read the words and examine the photo more closely.

"Sea Shanties. It's not exactly my kind of music, but this is a group of locals who make up a community choir; they sing shanties and maritime songs. I'm told they are quite good," Hamish said as the group paused in front of the poster. "Are you a fan of this music, Agent Stone?"

"Yes, my father would play Lightermen Sea Shanties throughout the house on weekends. The songs were always interesting to me," As he continued reading the printing.

"Well then, we shall give you something to remember London by instead of crime and spy craft. I will arrange for a car to pick you up at 5 p.m. We'll have dinner and enjoy some Sea Shanties at the pub. I hope you appreciate good beer or Scotch, as we have the best," he said, sounding slightly boastful.

"I would enjoy that very much; however, I don't drink, never have."

"Never?" Hamish said, surprised. "Religious or for health reasons?"

"Neither. These lips have never touched a drop. Just never had an interest," Stone replied, turning to walk on. Hamish raised his eyebrows but dropped the subject.

The room turned out to be an apartment that overlooked the MI6 building across the street. It boasted modern amenities and two bedrooms. Adjacent to the window was a small bar stocked with several unopened bottles of local Scotch, Russian Vodka, and Gin. Crystal glasses were neatly arranged in a semi-circle on the small mirrored table. Jacob picked up the bottle of Scotch, nodding his approval.

"I'll take care of these," Jacob said, smiling. Hamish returned an approving nod.

"If you need anything, dial 646, and you will be connected to our operator," Hamish explained.

"646…MI6," Jacob said with a smile.

"Very observant, Agent Westerly," Hamish commented.

"Is there a Cone of Silence we should use when discussing anything secretly?" Jacob said jokingly, referencing the American TV spy show 'Get Smart.'

"No, sir. We removed those last week in exchange for triple-pained windows with music piped in and weekly sweeps by our Q-branch," Hamish said, giving Jacob a wink. I will call when the car is out front." Hamish turned and left, shutting the door behind him.

"I need to contact the boss and let him know our travel plans for tomorrow," Stone said, removing his satellite phone. Jacob looked surprised.

"A Sat phone? Hamish said the phones here were secure."

"Maybe so, but one person knowing a secret is a secret, and two people make it a publication. We need to visit Massoudo's apartment in Hamburg tomorrow. And only our people need to know. They can set up the flight. I'll apologize to Hamish later." As he turned to speak on the phone.

Jacob found his suitcase lying on the bed. Very nice accommodations for a couple of G-Men, he thought. Two days on the job, and here he was in London, meeting super spies from MI6 and about to visit an authentic English pub. Right out of a book, he thought.

There were still a couple of hours before they left for a night of Sea Shanties, and Stone was determined to make the most of the time. He and Jacob sat at a table with the laptop in front of them, placing the three SD cards provided by Hamish on the table. Jacob inserted the first one into his laptop reader, and the computer screen displayed a file folder containing encrypted files.

As an extra precaution in case the three SD cards were corrupted, Jacob decided to copy the folder to his desktop.

Jacob double-clicked the non-descript folder. It opened, showing several dozen folders with numeric titles, making no sense of what they were identifying.

"Well, where do we start?" he said to Stone, who was concentrating on the screen.

"This one," pointing to a folder entitled "7877se". "It appears to be the only one with an alpha-numeric title."

Jacob navigated the mouse pointer over the folder and double-clicked it. Nothing. Then, a small window opened, and the lettering above it read, "Enter key." Jacob looked at Stone.

"Any thoughts?"

"Let's try the obvious. Type in Massoudo," Jacob slowly typed the letters into the space and clicked on enter. The folder disappeared as if immediately deleted.

"I think this will be a long night at this rate. Now what?" Jacob said with a sigh.

"Try another. Just pick one." Stone said.

Jacob selected a file that stood alone. The number 6476 is written below. He double-clicked. This time, for a brief moment, a high-resolution photo appeared, and then the words "enter key" appeared once again in the center of the screen with a blinking cursor.

"Wait a minute. I have an idea. What if I ran a screen recording program and then opened another file? The program records everything that appears on the screen in real-time. Then we could go back and run the screen video to get a frame of what the file is showing before it's deleted."

"Give it a shot. Right now, we have very few options, and we need to know what is so important about the information on this card." Stone said.

Jacob initiated the recording program and adjusted the settings to capture any image on the laptop screen. With a click on the black triangle in the corner, the timecode started running, indicating that the program was generating a video file of the screen. Jacob selected one of the initial files, labeled "1323," and double-clicked on its icon. The file briefly opened, but it vanished before Jacob or Stone could catch a glimpse, and a window appeared, prompting them to enter a key. Jacob pressed the stop button on the recorder, which opened a new window displaying the icon of the newly created video file. His heart raced as he clicked on the freshly generated file.

The screen appeared unresponsive initially, but then Stone noticed the timecode advancing. They realized they were watching a video of Jacob opening file 1323 rather than directly observing the laptop screen. The screen flashed briefly with the image from the file. Jacob pressed the stop button and used his cursor to rewind the video slowly. And there it was, captured by the program, only one or two frames of footage.

Jacob and Stone paused, examining the image closely. It depicted an old book, its spine made of brown leather with six raised bands. Unfortunately, they couldn't identify the book's contents or title from this photo alone. Nevertheless, the fact that the assassin had deemed it necessary enough to photograph intrigued them. Jacob attempted the same procedure and viewed a photo of a blue McLaren Speedtail. He recalled browsing luxury cars after receiving the funds from selling his ship. With a price tag of $2.3 million, he had concerns about becoming a target for carjackers associated with Colombian cartels. Consequently, he opted for a safer choice by purchasing a Tesla, which he would later regret.

What were the other photographs and documents? Jacob attempted to open a third file, but this time, the computer froze. Nothing would open. He rebooted the computer only to discover the folder was corrupted. This was some very advanced encryption software. But at least now they had an idea what the card contained.

"Should I email the card contents back to D.C. so the techs can work on it?" Jacob asked.

"Can you attach my Sat phone to your laptop? Stone asked while putting the phone down in front of Jacob.

"Sure, I can just attach a data line to it and log into the servers in D.C. Why is there something I should know?"

"I'm not sure who we can trust with this info. Someone has already been killed for the information, and we just need to cover all our tracks. Speaking of which, I spoke to the Assistant Director of FinCen. Bennett has us booked on the 6 am out of Heathrow to Hamburg."

Jacob had only seen Assistant Director Bennett when he came into the office for a preliminary meeting with Stone before heading off to Glynco at FLETC. Still, he heard about him from another experienced agent teaching at FLETC. Jacob and the Agent met at the pizza shop on base, and after several beers, Jacob got an earful from the Agent.

Jonathan Bennett, known as Jack to his friends and enemies, had been a seasoned intelligence officer in the CIA before coming to Treasury. He was a middle-aged man in his early 50s with a tall, athletic build. His short-cropped salt-and-pepper hair and blue eyes often reflected a mixture of cunning and determination. Despite his disciplined and focused nature, he has a dry sense of humor, which occasionally surfaces during moments of levity amidst the intensity of his work. Having served as the Chief of Station in Moscow, Bennett is well-versed in the intricacies of espionage, counterintelligence, and the geopolitical landscape. But he also had a dark side. No one could say what that was, but rumors suggested that he was allowed to transfer or be dismissed from the CIA, which led to his swift return home. Somehow, he was promoted to Assistant Director of FinCen, which ruffled more than one set of feathers. For now, he was the only one Stone was sharing information with, even though Stone wanted Bennett to think he was a team player, keeping MI6 in the loop.

The phone rang at precisely 5:00 p.m. The voice on the other end informed Stone that a car was waiting for them just outside the lobby doors. The two agents quickly grabbed their coats and umbrellas, preparing for any weather they might encounter outside. As they reached the lobby, they noticed Hamish standing by the car, smoking a cigarette. When he saw them approaching, he extinguished the lit cigarette and opened the rear door.

"Sea Shanty's await," he said with an upbeat tone.

"I'm looking forward to this," Stone said while entering the car. Having remembered the seating pattern outside Heathrow, Jacob took his position riding, shotgun in front. A woman was now driving. This one was much more outgoing than the last.

"This is Agent Olivia Hawthorne," Hamish said, introducing the young redhead woman who smiled at both Americans.

"First time in Great Brittan?" she asked Jacob while pulling out of the parking lot.

"Yes, I have always wanted to see your country, so this was pretty exciting,"

"And so, you decided Sea Shanties was the best way to experience English hospitality?" Olivia said with a glance and smile at Jacob. He was taken by her flame-red hair and command of the Audi in traffic.

"No ma'am, that was Agent Stone's interest; I'm more of a bagpipes guy," returning the smile. Olivia understood his humor.

"Please, it's Olivia. And I come from a long line of pipers," she said while glancing at Jacob. "Will you be with us for a while?" Stone glanced up at Jacob to gauge his response.

Jacob did not have to look in his visor mirror to know that Stone had his stare on the back of Jacob's head, awaiting the answer.

"Not quite sure at this time. We go where the information takes us," he said, looking out the window. The evening lights started coming on, and the traffic was picking up. Jacob could hear Stone and Hamish speaking at a low volume in the backseat. He could not make out the context of their conversation; however, Hamish, at one point, let out a loud reply.

"Ha, yes sir, I believe you are right," the two agents continued to speak.

As the car pulled up in front of the Gatehouse Pub, a line of people had gathered to gain access for the show. Olivia stopped the car directly in front of the door and turned off the engine. As they exited, a police officer approached the three men and a woman parking in a restricted spot. Olivia stepped up to the uniformed officer, removing her small black wallet and displaying it inconspicuously. The conversation was cordial and professional, with the officer displaying a dip of his cap to the agent, then taking a position near the car, giving his undivided attention as if being a personal attendant. Once in position, the officer nodded to the ticket taker standing at the entrance door. That motion provided an opening in the crowd for the agents to pass the fans and make a quick entrance to the building.

Upon entry, the agents handed their overcoats to a young lady who secured them in a room behind her. Olivia was given a small ticket for future identification of their garments. The four agents were escorted to a small table overlooking a stage at the end of the pub.

"This is very nice," Jacob commented, taking in the surroundings.

"This is one of the auditoriums, dating back to 1895. It was once a meeting room, a court, a Masonic lodge, and a jazz music club. Byron, Cruikshank, and Dickens once passed through its doors. Even your own Simon and Garfunkel performed here in the 60s." Olivia bragged.

"Ladies and Gentlemen, what can I get you to drink?" asked the young waiter as he handed dinner menus to each.

"Olivia?" Hamish looked at her.

"A G&T for me, thank you," referencing a Gin and Tonic.

"Gentlemen, what do you fancy?" looking at Jacob and Stone.

"Tonic with lime," Stone instructed.

"The same," repeated Jacob, not comfortable with ordering alcohol while on the company dollar. This got a small smile from the British side of the table.

"Very good. I'll be back shortly with any questions you have about dinner," the waiter said, closing his notepad and walking off.

Sea Shanty music played in the background as the crowds slowly entered the room, taking their seats. The agents sat, saying nothing and looking about the room. Jacob felt uncomfortable not speaking, and in an attempt to get the conversation going, he looked at Olivia.

"How long have you been at…" pausing as all eyes went to him, waiting if he would say the two letters and number they would prefer not to be blurted out in a crowd.

"The distillery?" Olivia interrupted before Jacob broached a word, he would later regret saying amongst unknown ears.

"Uh, yes. The distillery? Jacob caught on quickly.

"Several years. I find that this kind of work suits me quite well. I look for interesting, rare beverages worldwide and then tell others what I have discovered." She said with a slight upturn at the corner of her lips.

"And when she finds those rarities, I coordinate our team to visit and acquire them," Hamish said, looking directly at Jacob.

"Do you ever make your way to the United States?" trying to keep the topic alive.

"No, you have specialists in your country who know exactly what groups are distilling. But we do occasionally check in with our counterparts in America. We have more than enough work in the U.K. to keep us busy." Hamish explained. "And you? What got you into this line of work?"

"I helped, Cas…Ag…Uh, Mr. Stone, find some rare items that his distillery is interested in. I became interested in this line of work and applied for a job at his office. I'm the new kid on the block." Jacob smiled.

"That's for sure," Stone said, looking down at his plate.

"Well, you seem like a very bright young man, and I have no doubt you will have a long career ahead of you. Here's to your good luck in finding what you are looking for." Hamish lifted his drink that had just been placed on the table by the waiter. The others raised their glasses, taking sips.

After dinner, orders were placed with Jacob and Olivia having the first of their two-course dinner, pear stilton and walnut salad. Stone chose to start with the vegan mushroom croquettes. He had always enjoyed Spanish tapas, and this is where his eyes went first. Hamish had his favorite Padron peppers at the Gate House, usually mild in flavor and fried until blistered. Occasionally, a hot pepper would slip through, making eating them even more of a delight—a plate of glistening, steaming peppers.

For their second course, Olivia needed help selecting, eventually choosing the chicken, chorizo, and bean stew with buttered greens. Hamish and Stone decided on the beer-battered haddock, triple-cooked chips, peas, and tartare sauce. Pumpkin, one of Jacob's favorite flavors, selected the Delicia pumpkin, leeks, spelt, and hazelnuts with honey and mustard dressing.

Nearing the end of dinner, a group dressed in striped shirts reminiscent of old English sailors walked onto the stage. The lights slightly dimmed, casting a soft blue glow on the singers. As the night progressed, Jacob occasionally glanced at Stone quietly singing along with the songs. It was a side of Stone that Jacob hadn't seen before.

Suddenly, Jacob felt a slight movement on his leg. He realized it was Olivia's leg making contact with his. Slowly, he turned his head to look at her and found her already looking at him. Her raised eyebrow quickly lowered as she redirected her attention to the stage. Jacob couldn't decipher the meaning behind her gesture. Was she trying to convey something to him?

He couldn't help but think about how Olivia would discover in the morning that the two U.S. agents had left without even a word of thanks. She was intelligent, funny, and undeniably beautiful. He was interested in her, but at that moment, his thoughts were consumed by their dinner encounter. His heart raced, and he grew increasingly distracted, no longer fully engaged in the show.

After the show, they returned to the young lady who held their overcoats. Jacob made it a point to hand Olivia her coat, and she graciously thanked him before turning to leave. She seemed adept at maintaining her composure and keeping any potential signal between them.

As they exited the pub, rain began to fall, prompting them to hurry towards the waiting Mercedes parked right in front.

"Thanks for a wonderful night, Hamish and Olivia, I enjoyed the evening," Stone said.

"Our pleasure. It's not often that we have the honor of enjoying a night out with our American counterparts. I hope we'll have the opportunity to do this again."

Stone remained emotionless, fully aware that they would disappear without leaving a trace come morning. Jacob, on the other hand, kept his gaze fixed on the road ahead, his mind consumed with the events of the past few hours. Was Olivia attempting to orchestrate something, hoping they would extend their stay for several more days? Jacob stole a glance in her direction, committing the features of her face to memory in the slim hope that their paths would cross once more—an outcome he genuinely yearned for.

CHAPTER 5 (Hamburg)

At the apartment where Jacob and Stone were staying, there was no need for a traditional check-out process like in a hotel. Their departure before sunrise would go unnoticed by anyone in particular. Jacob utilized his UBER app to request a vehicle, scheduling it to pick them up at 5:30 am. A young lady in a beige BMW i7 series arrived at the front door of the building to meet them. The drive to Heathrow Airport was brief, taking only 30 minutes. Upon arrival, the agents checked in, appearing like ordinary American businessmen traveling on a weekday. However, the notable difference was that they were armed. With the discreet display of their identification and government-issued passports, they were granted access through a side entrance, bypassing security and entering the secure area without being detected by the general public. Stone remained at the gate, waiting for the boarding announcement for their flight to Hamburg, while Jacob purchased two cups of coffee from a nearby kiosk—one black and the other with a large amount of sugar. The caffeine provided the necessary boost to Jacob's energy levels for the early morning. Returning to Stone, Jacob handed him his coffee.

"We need to go to the next gate," Stone said, standing up with his carry-on and coffee. Jacob looked at him confused, as they were sitting at the correct gate.

"Cas, you know…" he could not finish his statement as Stone walked off without him. Jacob stood and quickly followed behind. They walked several hundred yards and turned into another crowded gate, where they took a seat. Stone, looking as if he was finishing a crossword puzzle on his folded newspaper, tapped his pen on the paper, looking confused.

"What do you think 31 across is?" Stone asked, handing the paper to Jacob. Jacob was taken aback. Stone had never shown any interest in or inclination toward crossword puzzles before. Irritated, Jacob glanced at clue 31 across, and suddenly, his heart started racing. In Stone's handwriting, there was a note that read, "We are being followed. Don't look around. We are going to miss our flight intentionally."

"Who knows? I hate doing these things," Jacob replied, trying to appear bored. The gate agent called for passengers who were in seats 44 and above to board the plane. Stone looked at his boarding pass and stood.

"That's us. Come on," Stone said to Jacob. Both agents stood in line with the other passengers, waiting to board. When they reached the ticket agent scanning passes, the machine flashed red. The ticket agent scrutinized their papers carefully.

"I'm so sorry sir but you are not on this flight. I believe your gate is two more in that direction, pointing to the end of the walkway. Looking confused, Stone examined the ticket.

"Oh my gosh, I apologize for the early morning confusion. Thank you," Stone apologized, taking back his ticket and walking away with Jacob following closely. As they made their way to the gate where their flight was scheduled to depart, they found the chairs unoccupied. The digital display only indicated the gate number without any further information. As they approached, they noticed a lone ticket agent standing behind the counter.

"Good morning, it appears we went to the wrong gate and missed our flight. Can we rebook on another?" Stone asked politely. The ticket agent typed into the computer, reviewing the possibilities.

"There is another flight leaving in 45 minutes from terminal 5C gate C53 if that would work?" the ticket agent asked Stone.

"Yes, perfect. Thank you," Stone said, glancing around as if about to address Jacob. He carefully scanned the nearby travelers, but there was no sign of the three men who had shown interest in their destination. The ticket agent printed out a document and handed it to Stone, and they swiftly made their way to their new terminal. Along the way, Stone managed to flag down an attendant driving an electric cart.

"Young man, excuse me. I really thought I could walk on my own, but the recent back surgery is saying otherwise. Any chance we get a quick lift to terminal 5C?" Stone acted as if in agony, holding his lower back and grimacing. The man driving the cart looked like he would be breaking some airport rule and hesitated momentarily.

"Certainly sir, let me help you on. My name is Geoffrey." The young man assisted Stone to sit beside him, while Jacob sat to the rear. They sped off, leaving anyone tailing them fast behind.

As they pulled up to gate C53, Stone slowly stepped from the cart while Jacob handed the driver a tip. The young man looked surprised but accepted the money, thanked them, and drove off.

"Very cool Agent Stone. I have to remember that one. Who do you think was following us?"

"I don't have a clue. Maybe MI6 caught on when we didn't answer the phone in our room. They could quickly check passengers and find our names."

"I would have thought they might approach us and say something. Unless they weren't MI6," Jacob said. Stone looked like he had asked himself the same question.

The flight to Hamburg was short, only one and a half hours, barely enough time to get comfortable and have a drink. Jacob closed his eyes for a couple of minutes, the tug of war in his body between needing to sleep and the inability to sleep on a plane battled inside him. Just as he was comfortably falling into a light sleep, the flight attendant welcomed them to the Hamburg International Airport. As Jacob and Stone exited the plane, Stone recognized a familiar face standing alone, awaiting their arrival.

"Agent Fuzzy Slippers," the man said with a smile, shaking Stone's hand. Stone looked partly annoyed at the name reference, shaking his hand while giving a small smile.

"John, how have you been?" Stone asked.

"Wonderful, Cas. I am back home, and all is well." The heavily German-accented man replied.

"This is Special Agent Jacob Westerly. Jacob this is Johann von Steinhardt from Interpol." As Jacob and Steinhardt shook hands.

"Please call me John, it is much easier," he replied. "You missed your original flight. Lucky for you. When I checked on your delay, I learned that your flight was returned shortly after take-off. Something in the cargo hold began smoking and set off alarms. One of my people is with the airport police, getting information, but it looks very suspicious. I'm surprised no one questioned why you missed your flight on that particular plane."

"We were being followed at the airport. Fortunately, some swift maneuvers enabled us to lose our unwelcome company. We managed to rebook this flight in a hurry. Can you please keep me informed about any findings from your team?" Stone inquired, his tone filled with a sense of urgency.

"I will check in with them shortly and update you," John assured Stone.

"I couldn't help but wonder, who exactly is Agent Fuzzy Slippers?" Jacob inquired a mischievous glint in his eye, fully aware that the mention of Stone's peculiar nickname held an intriguing tale within its folds.

"Ah, yes, another tale to be shared over a few beers," John chuckled, leading the way toward his car. As the trio strolled off, Stone shot Jacob a sidelong glance filled with irritation.

"How did John know we were here?" Jacob said in a low voice to Stone.

"I gave him a call last night after you hit the sack. He's an old friend, and I thought he might be able to grease the wheels for us," Stone replied. Jacob nodded approvingly and followed along.

After settling into John's car, they embarked on a journey to a downtown Hamburg hotel that had been prearranged for them by Jack Bennett from D.C. The hotel boasted a convenient no-contact check-in system, allowing Jacob and Stone to proceed directly to their room as directed in the text message. Jacob quickly configured his phone to serve as a digital key, following the hotel's instructions. The room itself was pleasant and tailored to cater to international guests. Instructions for the telephone and TV were available in English and German, ensuring ease of use for all visitors. A row of bottled water neatly lined the bathroom sink, offering reassurance that guests need not worry about consuming unfamiliar water sources and potentially encountering stomach issues.

"How do you know John?" Jacob asked Stone while John waited downstairs in the car.

"I met John at a class we both attended at Glynco. He was assigned to Interpol's Lyon office in France to participate in a Financial Investigation and Analysis Training program. Even though the course lasted just eight days, John and his wife stayed in the United States for a month, and my ex-wife and I took it upon ourselves to show them around. John harbors a keen interest in American Civil War re-enactments, so we decided to tour Gettysburg," Stone recounted with a hint of nostalgia in his voice."

"Is he working with us in Germany off the books?" Jacob asked.

"I'm not certain," Stone responded. "I made it clear to him that the mission was only to be disclosed to us and Bennett and that I wanted to keep it between us. He mentioned having a German Police investigator in his contacts, whom he claimed was trustworthy and dependable. I have faith in his judgment, so let's wait and see what he can do to assist us."

The two agents returned to John, who was waiting in his car, ready to assist. John drove a black Mercedes GLA 250 that comfortably seated the three men. He handed a tablet to Stone, who was seated next to him. Jacob watched as Stone examined photos and documents on the tablet.

"This is the man we've been looking for, Nabil Massoudo," the informant said, displaying a photo of a man on his phone screen. "He works part-time at a dry cleaner, ironing shirts. He has a preference for young men and chooses to pay for their company instead of dating them. Although he's been arrested before for minor offenses like drugs and vehicle problems, nothing substantial enough to bring him onto the radar... until now," he continued, pausing for a moment. He then proceeded to swipe over to the next page of photos, which contained several surveillance images of Massoudo conversing with various men on the street. "Each one of these men is a Russian intelligence agent, and Massoudo is providing them with information. He doesn't participate in dead drops; he meets with them and provides basic intelligence," he explained.

"Are the local cops or the BND interested in him?" Jacob asked from the back seat.

"Well, it does make one question why Massoudo is on the Russians' dance card, and yet we have received no information from the BND about his activities in Germany," John stated. "I presume this is why you wanted to keep our mission confidential between us," he added.

"Yeah, it seems like we're following leads that someone wants us to uncover," Jacob replied. Stone interjected, asking, "Are you absolutely certain about this German Police investigator you've brought on board?"

"Yes, I have a long history with him, and he has always come through for me. And very tight-lipped with the information I provide to him." John said with assurance in his voice.

John expertly navigated the local roads, and it took the team of agents approximately 45 minutes to arrive at the turnoff to Massoudo's last known address. Given that Massoudo had disappeared shortly after the hospital bombing, they had to assume that he might be present and uncooperative. As they parked down the street, a nondescript BMW pulled up behind them, driven by an older blonde man in a grey suit. He stepped out of his car and met John between the two vehicles. They shook hands and spoke for a few moments. Then, with a prearranged signal, John tapped on the rear of his car, indicating for Jacob and Stone to join them on the street. As they stepped to the rear of the vehicle, John introduced the U.S. agents.

"Special Agent Stone and Westerly, this is Kriminalpolizei Maximilian Schmidt, Criminal Investigator with In Hamburg, Police."

"Please, call me Max. And I believe the title in America would equate to your detective," Max said with a smile. As they shook hands, Jacob noticed several bandages on Max's hands. Max explained, "Oh, it's okay. I love to build furniture, and sometimes I overdo it."

Maximilian Schmidt is a man of many unusual and eclectic interests. Despite his serious profession, he is fluent in several languages, including Spanish and Mandarin, which he picked up during his travels. When he was not following criminals, furniture building and martial arts kept his mind calm and his body toned.

"Massoudo lives up the next block. How would you like to handle this? He has no current hold order, so he might not be very cooperative." Max said.

"In America, there is a police term called a 'knock and talk'. Sometimes, a bad guy will let the police in. Trying to appear they have nothing to hide. Once inside, who knows what might be in plain sight?" Stone said confidently.

"Alright, let's go knock and talk to him," Max said as they walked down the street.

As they made their way down the sidewalk, Jacob noticed that Nabil Massoudo's neighborhood within Speicherstadt was a relatively quiet area with a mix of residential and commercial buildings. The streets were lined with brick buildings, several stories tall, with large windows and ornate architecture. The neighborhood boasts a distinct European charm, featuring cobblestone streets and small squares lined with outdoor cafes and charming shops.

The four men stepped into a spacious and well-maintained elevator that smoothly ascended to the fourth floor. The back wall of the elevator was made of glass, offering a panoramic view of the river below. From there, they could see people strolling along the shore, relaxing on benches, and small boats leisurely drifting on the water.

As they approached apartment 410, Jacob and Stone unbuttoned their coats, ready to pull their handguns if needed. Two men positioned themselves on each side of the door, with the furthest man watching behind the man in front, ready if anyone came up to surprise them. They listened to any sounds in the apartment, but there were none. Max reached out and knocked on the door; it came ajar, which heightened the men's awareness. They paused, listening.

"Polizeibeamte, kommen Sie zur Tür." (*Police, come to the door.*) Max yelled.

No response. No movement in the apartment. Max yelled the command a second time. This time, he unholstered his Heckler and Koch P2000 handgun. This signaled the other agents also to arm themselves. They each took a defensive stance, preparing for any aggressive action coming from the apartment. Max, using his foot, slowly pushed the door open, once again yelling his command to come to the door. No response. He made a quick glance around the open-door jam, noticing debris scattered on the floor.

"I'm going to enter," Max advised the other men, each paying close attention to any activity in front of and next to them.

Slowly entering the luxurious apartment, Max had his gun in a slightly extended position, his sight fixed on the 180 degrees in front of him. The room was empty. Max cautiously moved in further, noticing the hallway directly to his right. He quickly stepped past the hall, swinging around and looking into the kitchen. Items on the floor and kitchen cabinets were opened. Stone and Jacob entered the room, covering the open area behind Max. Not officially allowed to carry a gun, John removed his Walther P5 from an ankle holster. His past training as a police officer in Germany afforded him the knowledge of the proper procedure to clear a room safely. He took a position covering the agent's back from the open door they had just entered. Slowly, Max and Stone moved down the hall, listening and ready for anyone who might quickly exit the side rooms. The bathroom door at the end of the hallway was open, with a large glass shower. This provided an unobscured view of the room, showing it was clear. However, two other rooms on each side of the hall still needed to be checked. Clothing and objects littered the floors as if the apartment had been ransacked. This made it difficult for the two-armed agents to make a stealthy advancement. Jacob remained at the end of the hall behind Stone and John, covering them in the event of a firefight. At the same time, John maintained a vigilant eye on the apartment door that he had closed for additional security.

Max slowly rounded the corner of the first room, using a tactical technique known as "slicing the pie," in which rounding a corner divided it into viewing areas like small pieces of an imaginary pie. This provided the officer with a fraction of a view that would detect the tip of a weapon or the tip of a toe protruding into the officer's view before the assailant knew they were there. Max completed the turn slowly and entered the room as Stone covered the unsearched room across from him. The room was trashed but clear, and Max turned his attention to the hall. This time, Stone proceeded to do the same technique; however, he noticed a pile of clothing protruding from the closet. He paused and then detected a slight movement under the clothes. Raising his hand with one finger to indicate someone was in the room, Max moved to the other side of the door frame, weapon trained on the closet.

"Du im Schrank, zeig mir deine Hände." (*You in the closet, show me your hands.*)," Max yelled. No movement came from the closet. This time, it was Stone giving the command.

"Police, show us your hands, now!" he said in a commanding voice.

Slowly, a pair of hands emerged from beneath the pile of laundry. Then the head of a terrified young man, his hair in a mess and tears running down his cheeks, peeked out of the pile, looking at the two-armed officers concealed behind the wall.

"Come out of the closet on your belly, hands in front of you." Stone instructed the young man.

The man, crying and scared, stretched himself across the floor as instructed. His face continued to look towards the agents. Dressed in a T-shirt and white underwear, he lay on the floor motionless. Stone ducked down, clearing himself from the line of fire. Max remained aimed at the closet from the doorway. Stone moved quickly, removing a pair of handcuffs. He holstered his weapon and placed the man's hands behind his back, cuffing them. Quickly pulling his weapon, he focused on the doors of the closet. He moved slowly and eventually was satisfied that no threat existed.

"All clear," Stone announced as he holstered his weapon. Standing the man up, he looked around the room, finding a robe on the floor and covering the half-naked, scared man. Max announced to Jacob and John that the area was clear. John locked the front door and secured his weapon, Jacob doing the same.

The man was seated on the bed as Stone and Jacob stepped in front of him. Stone moved a chair beside the man and wiped his face with a tissue he found on a nightstand beside the bed. The young man was starting to calm down, realizing these were officials and not adversaries looking to harm him.

"Do you speak English?" Stone said calmly. The man nodded, indicating he did. "What is your name?"

"Lukas," he said softly. Starting to gain his composure.

"I'll take the cuffs off if you promise to behave," Stone told him.

He once again nodded. Stone did a quick, cursory search around Lukas where he sat, double-checking there were no objects that could be used as a weapon if he had a change of heart. Once confident in the location, Stone removed his keys and unhandcuffed Lukas. He rubbed his wrists and wiped his eyes.

"What is your full name?"

"Lukas Müller, but everyone calls me Luke," he responded. John opened his notepad and wrote down the name, then exited the room.

"Do you live here Luke?" Stone asked. Luke looked down as if not knowing how to answer. Stone, knowing that Nabil Massoudo liked to frequent male prostitutes, knew the answer to the question.

"No, he hired me to spend a couple of days here," he answered, embarrassed by his reply.

"Luke, I'm not here to judge you. I want to make sure you are all right and safe. But I have some questions for you, if you are okay with that." Stone was showing a softer side that Jacob had not witnessed before.

Jacob slowly walked out of the room, leaving Max standing with Stone. Jacob and John began searching the apartment. The rooms appeared to have been thoroughly searched. Books that once rested on a large wall shelf were now scattered on the floor and open. Plastic containers in the kitchen had been opened, and their contents were dumped into the sink as if someone had been searching through them.

"What is the name of the person you were visiting?" Stone asked.

"He called himself Nabil. But I saw his name on a piece of mail. His last name is Massoudo." Bingo! Stone thought. This was confirmation that the man they were looking for was still living there.

"Do you know where he is?"

"When the men came, Nabil went out on the patio and disappeared," he pointed to the corner of the room in the same direction as the apartment patio. Jacob and Max, overhearing Luke's comment, moved to the balcony and looked over it. Four stories up, it was unlikely anyone would still be standing if they had dropped to the walkway below. A large copper decorative rain pipe was mounted just feet from the balcony. The pipe originated from a hole in the side of the building, just above the apartment, and ran to the bushes below. One of the wall mounts appeared to have been recently dislodged from the wall. The bushes below had been crushed. The damage to the bushes seemed to be the escape path of someone exiting Massoudo's apartment in haste.

As Stone interviewed Luke, he noticed the young man kept looking at a clock on the wall. At least, Stone surmised, he appeared nervous about the time.

"What were the men looking for when they broke in?"

"I'm not sure, but they kept saying 'Kamera' in Russian. I don't know what camera they were looking for. When they found me in the closet hiding, I was sure they would shoot me," Luke said while breathing hard.

"Yet they didn't. Why do you think that was, Luke?" Stone asked.

"I don't know. When they found me, one of them said in Russian, 'Что мы с ним делаем?' (*What do we do with him?*) The other guy said that the Praetorian only wanted the camera. The one man kept yelling at me about where the camera was. I thought they meant my camera," looking up at the clock. "I handed them the clock on the wall, and they looked at it and threw it back at me. They just tossed the clothes on me and left," Luke said with relief.

"The Praetorian." There was that word again. Stone pondered the name. Twice, they had heard it, and it made no sense. Stone recalled his younger days as a small boy and his collection of comic books. The Praetorian was a fictional character in Jupiter's Legacy's comic book series and its television adaptation, Super Crooks. He was a former superhero who had turned corrupt.

"Do you need to be somewhere, Luke? You keep looking at the clock," Stone said suspiciously. "What's the problem?"

Sam had entered the room, and he stepped up next to Stone, looking down at the nervous young man who was showing a slight bit of sweat on his brow.

"Lukas Müller," Sam said to the young man. "Born November 23, 2005, in Berlin. You have a history with us, and it's not just for prostitution." Sam said directly to Lukas.

Just then, John announced from the living room, "Cas, can I see you out here?"

"Excuse me," Stone said as he stood and walked down the hall to John and Jacob, who were standing with an old book in hand. John was fumbling with his phone, taking a photo of the item.

"Just what I thought," John said while turning his phone to Jacob and Stone.

Interpol designed the app on John's phone to identify online items of art that had been stolen. It allowed the user to search by category or country. The application enabled users to take a photo, and using artificial intelligence, it would compare the image to a vast database of missing and stolen items maintained by Interpol. In this case, there was a hit.

"Cas, why would a low-level thug and operative of the Russian Intelligence Service have a first edition folio of Shakespeare's work published 400 years ago? There are only 235 known surviving copies of this folio. The Folger Shakespeare Library in D.C. has 82 of them. I have no idea about the value of this one, but Sotheby's auction house in New York sold an original for 2.4 million U.S. dollars." John was holding the book, having already put on a pair of white cotton gloves to protect it from skin oils.

"Are you certain that's an original and not a forgery?" Stone asked.

John turned his phone towards Stone, displaying a nearly exact photo of a book on his phone that matched the one he held in his hand.

"It has the same markings; however, I won't know until my people examine it." He said as he removed a folded T-shirt lying on the floor, gently wrapping the book.

Stone returned to the room where Max had been speaking with Luke. In Max's hand was the wall clock Luke had been paying close attention to.

"Agent Stone, Luke has something he'd like to share with you," he said, turning to Luke before turning back to Agent Stone. "Luke, erzähl es ihm! (*Luke, tell him!*)"

"I've been taking photos of him," Luke said in a low voice, looking down at the floor.

"At who?" Stone was confused.

"Nabil. He doesn't know. If he finds out, he will kill me. Please don't tell him. The men who showed up were looking for him, but he got scared and ran away. As I said, I thought they wanted my camera," Luke said as he pointed to the clock Sam was holding.

Sam turned the clock over and removed what appeared to be a battery cover. A small, square electronic device was attached to the inside of the back. A small hole on the face of the clock, positioned precisely where the "o" was printed for the manufacturer's name, hid the camera's tiny lens. The camera was positioned directly in line with the bed Luke was sitting on. Stone suspected that Luke was blackmailing Nabil by photographing him in compromising positions with Luke.

"Why were you taking photos?"

"A man in town that I had a past relationship with approached me a few weeks ago and offered to pay me more money than I have made in a year. All I would need to do, is become friends with Nabil and take photos of him when we were intimate, you won't tell him, please you must not," Luke begged.

"Wasn't Nabil suspicious seeing this new clock mounted on the wall?" Stone asked.

"He let me live here in exchange for sex. I was allowed to sleep in this room. I put the clock up when I told Nabil that my cell phone was stolen. He didn't care and never suspected there was a camera." Luke explained.

"Who did you give the camera card to?" Stone asked with seriousness in his voice.

"I don't know his name. We would meet on the first and last Tuesday of the month at a café in town. I would give him the card, and he would give me a new one, along with an envelope of cash. I'm supposed to meet him tonight at 7 p.m." Luke explained.

"And these men that came to visit Nabil, what did they want? What were they looking for?" Stone pushed for answers.

"I don't know. Nabil looked out the window, but it was too late. The men had already started kicking open the door. It took them several kicks because Nabil had reinforced the frame with metal. By the time they got the door open, Nabil was gone. The men started tearing things apart. I begged them not to hurt me, but they didn't seem interested in me. They found Nabil's old laptop and then left. I was gathering my belongings to leave when I heard the door open again. I froze, terrified that the men had returned. But it was just you guys."

"What do you mean by an old laptop?"

"Nabil has a new one. A MacBook Pro. He never uses that old HP that they took. His laptop is behind the small bookcase next to the chair in the living room," Luke pointed towards the wall.

Stone checked with Jacob, who had been looking through the apartment. Other than the old book, he could not find anything of interest. If Nabil had the access key for the camera SD card, it was elsewhere. Stone glanced around the room and focused on the white Herman Miller chair in the corner.

"Take a look behind that bookcase," Stone instructed Jacob, pointing to the corner of the room.

Jacob walked over to the chair and bent over, looking behind the small two-shelf bookcase. He took a moment to reach between the back of the shelf and the wall. From behind, Jacob removed a small silver Apple MacBook Pro laptop.

"Eureka! Got it," Jacob exclaimed, holding up the computer.

"Why don't I take Luke to my station, get him photographed, fingerprinted, and cleaned up? When I get the café's name, I will text it to you, and we can meet there with Luke and see who shows up for the wall camera card," Max suggested.

"Good idea. Jacob and I will head back to our hotel and work on the file we have and this computer," said Cassius. Luke was escorted from the apartment to Max's station while the three other agents headed back to the hotel.

CHAPTER 6 (The water)

As the three agents approached the front of the hotel, where Jacob and Stone were guests, they observed three German Police vehicles and an ambulance parked, effectively blocking the sliding glass entry doors. The emergency lights on the vehicles flashed, yet there was no sign of anyone nearby. Inside the lobby, the guests appeared unaffected and carried on with their usual activities. The three employees behind the check-in counter provided diligent assistance to customers. The agents proceeded to the elevator and pressed the button for the tenth floor. Upon arrival, they disembarked and rounded the corner into the hallway leading to their assigned room. The incessant chatter of police radios filled the air, growing louder with each step. As they turned the corner to the hallway where Jacob and Stone's room was situated, they observed their hotel room door ajar, with several uniformed police officers positioned in the hallway, attentively gazing into the room. Jacob, Stone, and John slowed their pace as they approached, sensing the gravity of the situation. The officer nearest to them calmly raised his hand, signaling them to halt. "Bitte warten, Sie können in einem moment passieren," the officer said softly but sternly (*Please wait, you can pass in a moment*).

"This is our room. Is there a problem, officer?" Stone said.

The officer, understanding English, stepped towards the men as another uniformed officer joined him, keeping a view of the three men's hands. A third man in a suit stepped out of the doorway and approached the agents.

"You are the guests of this room?" He asked.

"Yes, the two of us are registered in this room, and this is a friend," Stone responded. Stone offered little information until he knew more about the situation in their hotel room.

"May I see all of your identification or passports?" the man in the suit asked.

"And who would we be giving this information to?" Stone asked, making it evident that he would not volunteer anything until he received an explanation.

"This is Detective Hanns Grubner of the Hamburg Police Kriminalpolizei," John said, stepping past Stone and extending his hand.

"Johann, I did not recognize you," the Detective said with a smile, shaking John's hand.

"Ich habe ein bisschen zugenommen, seit wir das letzte Mal zusammengearbeitet haben." (*I've gained a bit of weight since we last worked together.*) Patting his hand on his stomach. "Let's speak English," as he motioned to Jacob and Stone, indicating to Hanns that they did not understand German.

"Of course, Johann." Hanns nodded. "Welcome to Germany, where people die from our water," he said while pointing into the open door.

The three men approached the doorway cautiously, peering into the room. Inside, they saw the lifeless body of a young female dressed in a hotel room service uniform, lying face down on the floor. There was no sign of movement, and the medical personnel stood at a distance, having already examined the body and determined that further assistance was futile. Vomit was visible around the woman's mouth, and the partially wet floor indicated that water had spilled from an opened plastic bottle lying beside her. Jacob's gaze shifted past the woman and into the bathroom, where he noticed one bottle missing from the group lined up against the mirror.

"Gentlemen, I have your names from the front desk. Which of you is Cassias Stone?" he said, looking at his notepad. Stone raised his hand without saying anything. "Then you must be Jacob Westerly," looking at Jacob. "I must assume that if you are with Johann, then you must be Interpol or from the American Government, correct?" looking toward the agents.

Both Jacob and Stone introduced themselves, displaying their identification and badges. Hanns made a few notes in his pad before closing it and returning his attention to the men standing silently in front of him.

"Any idea what happened to her?" inquired Stone.

"I won't have a definitive answer until the pathologist conducts the autopsy, but based on the discoloration of her fingernails and lips, it's likely she was poisoned. It could be a substance like Novichok, which belongs to a family of rare fourth-generation chemical weapons developed during the Soviet era. For safety reasons, you won't be able to remain in this room as it needs to be decontaminated. Our technicians are currently inspecting your luggage to assess its safety, and we should have the results soon."

A plastic tarp was hung across the doorway, and medical personnel stayed inside the room while being tested for potential exposure. The woman's body was carefully placed in a specially designed body bag to prevent contamination to others. In an adjacent room, a portable mass spectrometer was set up to test the sample for any additional signs of contamination.

"We don't know if you were the target of the attack or if it was meant for someone who occupied this room before your stay," Hanns explained to the agents. "The hotel maids don't usually replace unopened water bottles, so it's possible that the bottle had been there for days. My partner is obtaining a list of guests from the past month, and we will conduct background checks on all of them. "John remained with Hanns as Jacob and Stone visited their new hotel room. Jacob looked at the bottles of water aligned along the sink in the bathroom.

"I don't think I'll be drinking any of these. Too many situations are occurring around us, don't you think?" Looking at Stone.

"You mean our inquisitive guests at the airport, the flight we were scheduled to travel on having a suspicious package nearly bringing it down, Russians searching the apartment of our suspect, and the maid being poisoned in our room? Not sure what you're saying, Agent Westerly," Stone said sarcastically.

Jacob opened Nabil's laptop on their desk. He removed a small hard drive from his bag and plugged it into the side USB port.

"First, I'll clone the hard drive just in case we have an issue when turning it on," Jacob explained to Stone.

The cloning process took a couple of minutes. In the meantime, Jacob turned on his personal cell phone, which he had kept turned off in his carry-on bag. Once active, the phone's display alerted Jacob of several missed calls. He dialed the voicemail number and sat listening.

"Son of a bitch," Jacob said as that statement caught Stone's attention.

When he was finished listening to the calls, he hung up the phone and sat at the desk quietly, looking down at his cell phone. He was in shock at what he had just heard.

CHAPTER 7 (Anya's back)

The door closed with a deafening sound that could rattle your teeth. The air inside carried a peculiar blend of disinfectant and pepper spray, remnants of earlier incidents that served to assert control over the criminal underbelly. This facility, ADX Florence in Colorado, was notorious for its unrelenting illumination, which never allowed for complete darkness. Referred to as a Supermax prison, it housed the most dangerous criminals within the Federal penitentiary system. So, how did a young and seemingly innocent Russian girl find herself here? She stood accused of murdering another woman and orchestrating the attempted murder of her ex-husband, now a Federal Officer working with the Financial Crimes Unit of the Treasury Department, aboard a luxurious mega yacht. Officially, there were no women incarcerated at ADX, except for Anya. Isolated in a separate wing, she had no contact with male prisoners except for one inmate who had tried to exploit Uncle Sam and paid the price. Anya felt a kinship with this person, or as they say, "My enemy's enemy is my friend". It was a tale from another era that Anya wished she could forget. However, the ghosts of past nightmares continued to haunt her, conjured each time she succumbed to the allure of her former life—a life of opulence, wealth, gourmet meals, and the finest Russian vodka.

The discharge officer slipped a document and a pen through a small opening at the bottom of the bulletproof glass window. Anya signed the document and slid it back, sealing her fate once again.

A brown paper bag containing its contents was placed inside a hinged metal box in front of the officer. Once closed, the recipient on the other side could open the drawer. This design prevented any person or object from being sent in the opposite direction into the prison's control room. Inside the bag were a pair of deck shoes, women's underwear, shorts, a shirt, sunglasses, and a small wallet containing various jewelry items, including a ruby necklace. The necklace held sentimental value, given to her by her adoring father on her twenty-first birthday—a lavish display of love costing sixty thousand dollars. These were all the personal belongings Anya had on her when she was apprehended by the U.S. Marshals while opening the door to her San Francisco townhouse. She never even made it inside. Taken down at gunpoint by men the size of linebackers, clad in bulletproof vests, her wrists swiftly restrained behind her back in handcuffs, after being body slammed to the floor from a foolhardy attempt to escape. Still sporting the scare on her nose from that eventful night.

She turned and walked out of the prison door; her face devoid of emotion. Thirty steps led her to a metal rotating turnstile that led to another building with an automatic sliding door. Once she had passed through the second building, she would reach the parking lot. This area was unfamiliar to her. The Supermax facility was designed so inmates never knew their exact location. During her time in the facility, when she was occasionally escorted from her cell to the mailroom, Anya tried to determine her direction of travel by observing the sunlight streaming through small windows. She noticed the shadows and how the angle changed with each passing month. Meals were delivered to her cell, and any exercise was done in the confined space where she spent 23 hours a day alone. Everything in her cell was made of grey concrete, except for the stainless-steel sink and toilet combination. Photos and drawings were not allowed on the walls of her cell. She possessed two photos: one of her parents standing on a beach, smiling at the camera, and the other a wedding photo of her and Jacob on the bow of a ship, with Diamond Head, Hawaii, in the background. Occasionally, she was permitted to go to the yard with a few other inmates, but they were forbidden from communicating, and she risked being shot by a tower guard if she approached any other inmate. She was here for a reason, not due to behavioral issues like ninety percent of the other inmates in the facility. However, within these walls, she could plan and coordinate things through a network of correctional officers handsomely paid by individuals in her cabal. Someone was ensuring her safety while also keeping a close watch on her.

As she exited the final building, a black Mercedes SUV was parked, ready for her departure. Approaching the vehicle, a young man in a suit received her package and opened the back door without uttering a word.

"How long until we get to the plane?" she asked the driver.

"Thirty minutes, ma'am,"

"How is he," looking at the driver's rear-view mirror.

"Not well. He's pretty sick."

When the SUV arrived at the airport runway, Anya boarded the plane and settled into an unoccupied seat with no other passengers. The pilot of the Bombardier Global 7500 smoothly lifted the aircraft off the ground, the twin General Electric Passport 20-thrust engines gently pushing Anya back into her seat. As Anya gazed out the window, she wondered if she would reach her destination in time during the long flight.

CHAPTER 8 (Bada-bing)

"Special Agent Jacob Westerly for Robert Miller, please."

The phone line was put on hold as Jacob awaited the California Deputy Attorney General (DAG), who had overseen the plea deal with Anya. Jacob had several questions for the DAG, who had earned a reputation for pursuing criminals and employing unconventional tactics to secure convictions. Miller, a local California Deputy AG, had convinced Federal authorities that housing Anya in the ADX facility in Florence, Colorado, instead of a California penal colony, was necessary to prevent her from contacting Russian assets, either to repay Jacob or to collaborate with her father Peter, who operated from Hamburg, Germany. However, Miller would soon realize that this decision was a mistake.

"Agent Westerly, Robert Miller," the Deputy AG had a deep, commanding voice. "You are a very hard man to get a hold of; you must have gotten our dozen or so voicemail messages."

"I understand Anya Stanislavski is being released, why?" Jacob got right to the point.

"She filed with the appellate court to reverse her conviction, and it was granted..." he tried to explain, but his explanation was cut short.

"Reversed her conviction? How?" Jacob's voice escalated. "The guy who shot her was caught on video and arrested by the San Francisco detective. He even confessed that Anya orchestrated the whole thing to eliminate Lisa. And let's not forget how she attempted to kill me on the ship." Stone sat at the table, attentively listening and examining the photos on Jacob's laptop. Despite his extensive experience, Stone chose not to intervene and instead allowed Jacob to express his frustrations and gain valuable insight into the complexities of the criminal justice system —a journey that all law enforcement officers undergo. Ideally, one would assume that once a judge hands down a sentence, all the perpetrators remain in custody. However, reality often proves otherwise, as various forces come into play, sometimes backed by seemingly endless resources capable of swaying the course of justice. Whether it's an influential oligarch whose daughter is behind bars or a president granting pardons to individuals who have placed themselves in compromising positions to assist others, premature releases happen all too frequently.

"Yes, you're correct. The evidence against her was compelling, which is why she ultimately accepted the plea deal. However, someone must have persuaded her to involve her father at some point. According to Anya's statements, she portrayed herself as an unwilling participant acting under her father's orders. She claimed to be a mere pawn in their scheme, with her father's henchmen coercing her into cooperation by threatening your life and hers should she refuse. In her written account, Anya explicitly denied pulling the trigger that ended Lisa's life, emphasizing that her father and his two accomplices concocted the plan to throw you overboard on the ship." Miller explained.

"So, get the three Russians who were arrested and flip them with offers of a smaller sentence for cooperating," Jacob instructed.

"We considered that possibility and dispatched agents to interview them extensively. However, the individual who pulled the trigger was fatally attacked in prison. The other two met similar fates—one was discovered hanged in his cell, while the other was killed during what appears to be a premeditated altercation among inmates in the yard. Sadly, all of our potential witnesses have died. Additionally, there was an inmate who shared a cell with one of the Russians in the same facility, and he attempted to gain some leverage by informing the authorities that he had been told the same story, implicating Peter Stanislavski as the mastermind. As it stands, it's essentially Anya's word against... no one." He explained.

"The video of the two guys throwing me overboard counts for nothing?" Jacob asked.

"Anya doesn't dispute what was seen on the video, but as I said, she claims her father would have had her killed if she did not go along with it," Miller said, sounding annoyed he was repeating the same information.

"And no one thought to contact me, the victim. Great," Jacob said sarcastically.

"When we couldn't reach you by your personal cell phone, we reached out to your boss at Treasury. They said you were on assignment overseas and unavailable, but they would relay the information as soon as you surfaced. I assume that was not done?" Miller asked.

"Thank you for the update, Mr. Miller. Do you have any idea where Anya is?"

"I understand that she was released three days ago from the ADX facility in Colorado and boarded a personal jet that did not file a flight plan."

"I need to see her prison file. Everything. Nothing removed and nothing redacted. Can you make this happen?" Jacob asked Miller in a stern voice transmitting his "I'm not fucking around" attitude.

"I'll have it sent to your office, and they can relay it to you. Does that work?" Miller asked.

"No, if your office could make the copies and send them directly to my Sat phone," Jacob turned to Stone, who scribbled down the number, handing it back.

"Got it, the file should be to you in a couple of hours," Miller assured Jacob.

Jacob pressed the end button on his phone. His facial expression and body language transmitted his anger at the situation. He sat looking at the wall, speechless.

"I cannot believe this happened. Anya has been released and is off to who knows where," Jacob said with disgust.

"These things happen. Welcome to the job. You learn to grow a thick skin and take the position of, if they release them, I'll just put them back in," Stone said in a low voice, keeping his attention on the laptop screen and examining images of the few items recovered from the SD card.

"You're right. Even though my girlfriend and I were the victims, I just need to move on and make sure the next time Anya goes to prison, her father joins her," Jacob said while opening the laptop seized from the apartment.

Nabil's laptop powered on effortlessly, while Jacob found himself lacking the necessary login password. If the computer had been equipped with a self-destruct mechanism, entering an incorrect password three times would result in a complete freeze. To avoid this, Jacob employed a sequence of commands he had acquired while attending an Apple security class for the Treasury. This particular course took place at the Apple Campus in Cupertino, California. Jacob's return to California for training provided him with valuable learning opportunities and allowed him to reconnect with old acquaintances at Citation Software. His stay at the Juniper Hotel in Cupertino granted him the cherished routine of indulging in donuts at Donut Wheel on DeAnza Blvd, a morning and sometimes evening ritual. He relished the maple bars and coffee, dedicating an hour to reviewing lessons on his laptop while savoring the delectable pastries. Aware of the importance of preserving the laptop's contents, Jacob had taken the precaution of backing up the hard drive to a portable device, thereby ensuring he could examine the computer without the fear of losing any data.

He sat for a moment, recalling the specific directions to override the password protection on the Mac. He slowly typed in REDACTED. The screen paused and then provided the message, Enter a new password. Jacob entered a series of letters, numbers, and symbols he used for high-level encryption. The desktop image of the screen opened. The image depicted a tanker ship at sea. The photo was taken from the bow of the ship facing the stern.

Various files on the computer were examined. One, in particular, drew Jacob's attention: a one-sentence document written in the Amharic language, an Ethiopian Semitic language spoken by over fifty-seven million people in Ethiopia.

The page contained one sentence: ጨለማ ፍሊት. A quick Google search translated the sentence as "Dark Fleet."

"Hey, Cas, does the term Dark Fleet mean anything to you?" Jacob asked.

Stone looked up at his young agent, who was sitting with the laptop open. He was familiar with this term, and Treasury had several discussions with Naval Intelligence and the CIA about a Dark Fleet.

"The Dark Fleet consists of a large number of vessels owned or operated by various companies tied to criminal organizations that profit from the illegal trade of sanctioned oil. These tankers employ fraudulent documentation, disguises, or other tactics to evade detection and seizure. They generally do a cargo transfer in the middle of the ocean with their AIS systems turned off. Then, the loaded ship makes its delivery, and the money is exchanged. The problem with this activity is that it can destabilize the global oil market. Russia pumps much of its oil onto these tankers to circumvent the sanctions. The U.S. and its allies have had a hard time finding out where the ships are and when the transfers will be made," Stone explained.

A knock on the hotel door interrupted Stone's explanation. Jacob opened the door and found John pushing a luggage cart with Stone and Jacob's bags.

"Did you order bag service?" John said with German humor, "All bags are clean and good to go," as he pushed the cart into their room. "Max contacted me; he has Luke all cleaned up and wearing a wire so we can hear the conversation. He will meet us at the café around 6:30 p.m. to get in place. And I thought you might like to know that the bomb set off at the hospital killed the Chief of Security for an oligarch named Peter Stanislavski. He's been living in Hamburg for quite some time."

Jacob stopped placing their bags on the bed and turned to John with a look of surprise. He glanced over at Stone, who knew exactly what Jacob was thinking. Stone recognized this name from Jacob's past.

"Peter Stanislavski?" Jacob said with a tone of surprise.

"Yes, have you heard of him?" John asked.

"I was married to his daughter, Anya. She tried to kill me on Peter's orders."

"He is currently in a hospital recovering from a poison he contracted from his shaving razor. This bodyguard was leaving the hospital to recover it when his auto blew up," John said without emotion.

Jacob sat thinking for a moment. "All the pieces are starting to align," he thought.

"We need to see him, Cas," Jacob said, turning his attention to the Senior Agent.

"I agree, we need to interview him, if he'll talk. But first, we need to find out what Luke's handler knows. That might give us leverage over Peter when we go to the hospital," Stone explained.

John had agreed to drive the agents to Café Kostbar on the corner of Rosenhofstrasse and Susannenstrasse in downtown Hamburg. This quaint little café offered an ideal vantage point for conducting surveillance on a subject. Adjacent to the café was a one-way street, featuring outdoor seating that included picnic-style tables and benches. The street was flanked by parked cars on both sides, providing ample cover and concealment. This setup allowed the team to maintain a short distance while remotely listening and retain control in case the subject attempted to flee or, in the worst-case scenario, engage in a shootout.

Each agent was equipped with a communications earbud that also contained a noise-canceling microphone. The agents wore soft clothing to blend in. Each sat at a table; Stone read a newspaper, and Jacob fiddled with his phone. John positioned himself down the street on the opposite side of Rosenhofstrasse, covering the escape route on that side. Max provided a cover team in 3-man units around the area of Susannenstrasse. The cover team arrived an hour early to watch for anyone arriving and appearing to loiter. Their job was to provide backup in the event things turned into a shit show and bullets started flying. If all went well, Luke would hand over the envelope containing a small SD card. Once the handler gave Luke the envelope with the money, that would be the signal for Max and his team to move in and grab the handler. He would be quickly patted down for weapons, handcuffed, and placed into an unmarked van pulling up next to them. If all went well, they should be at the local police station a few minutes after contact.

Close to 7:00 p.m., the team's Comm system picked up the voice of Luke and Max in the area. Max explained the plan to Luke again, and Luke assured Max he could do this. All team eyes were on Luke as he entered the café and purchased coffee and pastry. He walked outside and picked a table further down the walkway, sitting on the outside bench facing the road. Max preplanned this, as Luke had explained that the handler liked to sit and chat for a few minutes.

This would force him to sit on the table's far side with his back against the café, making it hard to escape when people approached.

Several minutes passed when a man dressed in sweatpants, tennis shoes, and a T-shirt, covered by an unbuttoned shirt, approached Luke. His left hand remained in his pocket, while his right was visible. Stone immediately recognized the mode of dress, reminiscent of the Sparrows—assassins associated with the Marcos regime in the Philippines. During his early years, Stone received training on these assassins who targeted police officers patrolling the streets. They would conceal a semi-automatic pistol in the waistband of their sweatpants, with one pocket cut open at the bottom. By keeping their hand in the pocket, their fingers would extend through the opening, providing support for the end of the barrel. With a swift upward motion, the gun would be propelled into their other hand, ready to fire within a fraction of a second.

The man purposefully avoided sitting with Luke and instead positioned himself on Luke's right side, engaging in conversation. Stone spoke quietly, uttering the word "assassin," hoping the teams would understand the urgency and take action. At that moment, the man began to move his left hand within his pocket, causing Stone to fear that a weapon was about to be revealed. Reacting swiftly, Stone stood up and drew his weapon, startling Luke in the process. To his surprise, Luke turned quickly, inadvertently colliding with the man's legs and momentarily throwing him off balance. The gun in the man's waistband flew past his right hand, landing on the table just out of his reach. With all the teams now in motion towards the target, the man realized he was outnumbered and that retrieving the gun would only result in certain death. Cornered and desperate, he resorted to the instinctual response of all criminals—he ran.

The man weighed his options and ultimately decided to dash across the street with a swiftness that would have impressed even a professional track runner. Skillfully, he leaped onto the hoods of parked cars, smoothly landing on one foot before propelling himself forward along the deserted sidewalk. The German intelligence teams involved in the operation dispersed in different directions, utilizing their knowledge of the streets and their awareness of the obstacles ahead. Jacob, closely trailing the man, mirrored his path from the opposite side of the parked cars. Few pedestrians crossed their path, but those who did were caught off guard and swiftly found themselves on the ground. The runner maintained his balance and velocity, swiftly approaching the upcoming turn at the end of the road.

Jacob had decided early in the foot pursuit to holster his weapon and not chance an accidental discharge if he attempted to carry it. In the back of his mind, he decided that if the runner paused at any point, he would unholster his semi-automatic gun and be ready if the runner produced another weapon. Having known this area from their youth, the German officers ran parallel down the street just west of Jacob on Schulterblatt.

As the man came to the intersection, preparing to run north, his attention fixed on cars coming towards him, he never saw the officers to his left. The lead officer had the striking power of an American football linebacker. When a linebacker hits someone full force, it can be a jarring and intense experience, like being hit by a speeding truck; it can knock the wind out of you and leave you feeling disoriented and vulnerable. The runner, who could no longer escape, lay face down on the pavement, trying to catch his breath. Quickly handcuffed and placed in the back of the waiting German Police van that had been following him down the street, the man was driven away quickly as onlookers stood and captured video on their cell phones. Moments later, John and Stone pulled up with Luke in the backseat. Jacob took his place in the empty seat.

"Bada-Bing, and that's how we do it!" Jacob, feeling the adrenaline rush, jokingly commented as the vehicle drove off.

CHAPTER 9 (Old flames, new names)

Jacob's phone rang while Stone, John, and Luke were driving. Everyone was winding down from an exciting evening. The caller ID identified the caller as Kriminalpolizei.

"It's Max," Jacob announced to the others.

"Westerly here," trying to sound professional.

"Jacob, it's Max. Wow, what a fun day, catching bad guys together. But I have some bad news and some not-so-bad news," Max said, trying to soften the blow.

"Let's hear the bad news," as the others in the car became curious.

"The man Agent Stone nearly shot was an asset for your CIA. He was trying to find out what Nabil was doing, photographing the hospital, so he decided to use a source and see if blackmail would work. When he saw Agent Stone reaching for a weapon, he thought it was Nabil's people. We checked with your people and they are on their way to debrief the man, who by the way is Santino Cruz," Max paused for any questions.

"CIA? But he had a gun set up like a Filipino assassin.

"His dad was a highly trained assassin working for the Alex Boncayao Brigade outside Manilla in the 1980s. Santino was raised around the killings and his father's stories about how Santino would be a man one day and follow in his footsteps. He became disillusioned with all the Marxist bullshit, eventually meeting a young Filipino girl that turned him into a CIA asset. He made good money and never had to kill anyone, well at least none that we know of. As for that SD card, he was there to collect, nothing on it but porno shots of Luke and Nabil, nothing useful. I will send you copies just in case you like to look at this stuff," he said jokingly.

"If that was the bad news, what is the good," Jacob hesitated to ask.

"You asked me to have our airports watch for any unusual arrivals. We had a personal jet land a few hours ago at the Hanover airport outside of Hamburg. There was a single female passenger. Our customs agents questioned her even though she had a Cypress passport. Her name was Anastasia Stanislavski, she claimed that her reason for the visit was her sick father who was in the Vincent Hospital in Hanover. Her father had been transferred here from the Martin Luther Hospital in Berlin once he was stable. The same one where the car bomb exploded."

Jacob felt a slight wave of nausea washing over him. Perhaps it was due to the surge of adrenaline coursing through his veins, or maybe it was the fact that he had heard Anya's name mentioned twice within twenty-four hours. She seemed to linger in his thoughts, haunting him like a bad serving of gas station sushi. He pondered the reasons behind their paths intersecting again. Was it a coincidence that they were conducting business in the same country? Or did Anya have ulterior motives, with Jacob being her intended target? Seeking relief from these unsettling thoughts, Jacob turned to John and asked if he would be willing to take the wheel, driving him and Stone to the hospital in Hanover once they had dropped off Luke at Nabil's apartment.

"Peter Stanislavski, no problem. I haven't seen Peter for years," John said as he drove on.

"How do you know Stanislavski?" Stone asked.

"Years ago, Interpol had been working on human trafficking cases using oil tankers as the transportation method. All the ships belonged to Stanislavski's Oil company. When the war in Ukraine broke out, he had 15 ships in his fleet. Today, he has over 100. Who would benefit from his oil company being able to move more sanctioned oil? As for the human trafficking charge, he let a couple of his managers take the fall, and his company paid a few million dollars in fines. And you can bet the Kremlin put out the money to cover the fines. Peter has low friends in high places," John said in jest.

The three agents parked their vehicle in a nearby lot, taking a moment to observe the hospital from a distance. They noticed several unoccupied black SUVs parked at the curb. As they approached the entrance and pushed open the double glass doors, a pleasant surprise greeted them—a sweet fragrance of flowers wafted through the air. It was a refreshing departure from the typical clinical scent of disinfectant that permeated hospitals.

John approached the information desk, being the only member of the group fluent in German. He inquired about the room of Peter Stanislavski, which immediately drew the attention of several well-dressed young men lingering around the entrance area. The three agents noticed the men's gaze fixed upon them, prompting them to stay alert. The desk attendant informed John that the entire fourth floor was reserved and that they would need permission to access it. John confidently displayed his Interpol ID to the attendant, who promptly handed him a plastic pass card without further questioning. As the agents proceeded towards the elevator, two of the men who had been observing them began walking closely behind the group. Sensing this, Stone stopped and turned around calmly.

"It's okay, boys. We've got it from here. Go get some coffee," Stone said, extending his badge and ID to the man in the lead.

The man hesitated, seemingly contemplating whether to confront them. Stone remained still, not making any sudden movements, awaiting the man's decision. Eventually, the man chose to turn around and walk away, with the other man following closely but keeping a watchful eye on the agents.

"Good decision," Stone muttered under his breath.

The elevator opened to a hallway where several men in suits stood, staring at the agents. The men on the first floor had apparently warned the men that Government Agents would visit. One man stepped forward.

"I am the head of security; how may we help you?" The man asked Stone.

"Oh, you must be Serge's replacement. Sorry for your loss," he paused, "Peter?" Stone asked as if reminding the man why they were there.

The man hesitated briefly, casting a glance at Stone before continuing down the hallway. The three men, Stone, Jacob, and John, followed closely behind while the other sentries observed them with stoic expressions. When they reached the room, the man paused, and a soft voice was heard from inside. He nodded in response to the voice and stepped aside, allowing John to enter first, followed by Stone and Jacob. Throughout the interaction, his focus remained on Stone and then shifted to Jacob, clearly displaying his disfavor towards the law enforcement officers in his presence.

The room had been stripped of all additional beds and hospital equipment, except for a few monitors positioned near a larger bed resembling one found in a luxurious, well-appointed home. A frail older man with thinning gray hair occupied a large recliner beside the bed. Intravenous tubes, along with a catheter bag, were connected to him. He was dressed in silk pajamas, adorned with a robe and slippers. His complexion appeared pale and feeble, displaying the aftermath of enduring weeks of agonizing torture induced by a nerve agent his body was battling to overcome. His eyes drooped slightly, revealing the weariness of his spirit.

"Johann von Steinhardt, it has been a while since we last met. Are you still playing policeman?" Peter said sarcastically, knowing that John was still active in Interpol.

"Hello Peter, oh, you could use a shave. Wait. That's what got you here in the first place, wasn't it?" He felt good that his wit did not let him down. "I brought some guests who would like to speak with you," he said as he stepped aside.

"Agent Cassius Stone, your reputation precedes you, Agent Stone." Peter sat there, looking at Stone with a slight grin.

"Yours does also. After you tried to kill my Agent, I did a lot of research into you," Stone said with a bit of sarcasm in his voice.

"Ah, remember Agent Stone, he was not 'your agent' at the time. He was my son-in-law." Peter announced as if proud of Jacob.

Peter tilted his head to one side as if trying to look around Stone. He clapped his hands together as if excited to see Jacob standing in the background.

"Jacob, Jacob, please come forward. I am so sorry. Where are my manners, Agent Westerly? It is finally an honor to meet you. I am so sorry I could not attend the wedding, but I do want to thank you for taking care of my little girl. I know things did not turn out for the best; however, I believe you are a good man, and the two of you would have been a wonderful couple."

Jacob not showing any emotion. Peter's excitement sent him into a coughing fit. Neither of the three agents budged an inch to assist, as they stood there examining the man who was in stress. Two nurses quickly came in to assist; however, Peter waved them off, drinking some water from a nearby glass. He sat for a moment, catching his breath.

"So, what do you want from me? What is so important that a couple of Treasury Agents and their Interpol lap dog feel it necessary to travel halfway around the world, just to stress out an old man," breathing hard and annoyed with the people standing in front of him.

"We just wanted to deliver our condolences on the loss of Sergey. Why someone wanted to blow him up and, at the same time, send a guy to photograph it is the question that we thought you could enlighten us on," Stone asked.

"Gentlemen, I do not know. Sergey was like a son to me. He was going back to my villa for the razor that delivered this poison to me," his hands touching the bandage on his cheek. "I know who it wasn't, the people I do business with. They are loyal and would not bite the hand that feeds them," he said without emotion on his face.

"You have several more ships in your fleet. Is business that good, with the war running in your backyard?" Stone asked.

"People need oil. My company only moves legal oil. However, your government likes to take things in the name of justice from a country that is doing nothing more than recovering what has been ours for decades. If Canada invaded the United States and took your Wyoming and Montana, would you not fight to get it back? But no, you take my beloved Anastasia Dream without any reason. Is that justice, Mr. Stone?"

"It's Agent Stone. And I have no interest in debating history with someone like you. We want the items stolen from the allies returned. And if that means putting pressure on you and your company personally, well as your daughter said to Agent Westerly before having him thrown into the ocean, how does it feel to be a pawn in a much larger game," Stone, feeling as if he had just check-mated the old Russian sitting in front of him.

Just then, a voice came from behind the group, standing in the doorway.

"Hello Jacob,"

Sensing Jacob's presence, Anya deliberately chose an ensemble that exuded both style and seduction to capture his attention. Her attire consisted of a knee-length, form-fitting black dress with a plunging neckline that subtly hinted at her alluring décolletage. The dress skillfully embraced her curves, accentuating her figure with an understated allure. Complementing the ensemble, she adorned herself with high-heeled black stiletto pumps, adding height and elegance to her overall look. Around her neck, she wore a delicate silver necklace that gracefully brushed against her exposed skin, drawing attention to her collarbone and further enhancing her appeal.

Jacob was not sure how to react. He was at a loss for words to a woman who, only a couple of years earlier, assisted two Russians in his near demise. They stood looking at each other for a moment. Stone and John watched Jacob's reaction.

"Anastasia my love, I am so pleased you could make it," Peter said with excitement.

Anya strolled past Jacob, her presence near enough for him to catch a fleeting whiff of her Gardenia perfume—the same fragrance she wore on the day they shared their first kiss. Memories flooded his mind, overwhelming his thoughts before he could fully process them. She moved gracefully, almost gliding across the room, leaning over to warmly embrace her father with a hug and kiss. The other men in the room took notice of their interaction and exchanged glances. Jacob found himself unsure of how to navigate his emotions at that very moment.

"This is a wonderful day, is it not? My lovely daughter and my almost son-in-law are together in the same room. If the doctor had not forbidden it, I would be opening a fine Russian vodka to celebrate," Peter said as he lay in bed holding Anya's hand.

"I think our visit is finished," Stone said as the agents turned to leave. Walking down the hall, Jacob trailing behind, a voice called out.

"Jacob, can I speak with you for a moment, alone?" Anya asked, standing feet from her father's hospital door.

Jacob wondered if the visit was appropriate, so he glanced at Stone for guidance. With a nod from Stone, Jacob understood that he had no objections to the visit.

"We'll stand by at the elevator," Stone said as he and John turned to walk away.

"What do you want?" Jacob was cold and direct to the point.

"Jacob, I did not want us to meet again with these kinds of dark clouds over us," Anya said as she took a few steps closer, her voice low and trying to sound sincere.

"You tried to have me killed, Anya. I loved you with all my heart, but it was worth nothing. You used me and then threw me away like trash. How am I supposed to feel?" Jacob could feel his blood pressure rising.

"I was not responsible for that. I was scared for my life and doing what I had to do for survival. I never wanted to see you die. A future with children and seeing the world was what I had imagined," Anya pleaded with him.

"You know what I imagined? A life vest, while I was floating in the ocean watching the ship sail off with you aboard, in a comfortable bed, drinking vodka, while I nearly froze to death in the water. I still have a scar on my lip where you bit me, with the hope that my blood would attract sharks and let me die quickly. Isn't that what you said before your goons threw me overboard?" Jacob was breathing hard, his nostrils flaring.

"I'm sorry, Jacob. If I could go back in time, I would change everything that happened between us. Except for the good times, and we had quite a few," she smiled as if thinking about the past.

"And let's not forget Lisa. You had your people shoot her in the head so she wouldn't be in your way. What kind of a monster does that?" Jacob felt as if he had been holding this inside for so long, and here it was, bubbling out on the hospital floor where people listened while pretending to work.

Standing at the door to Peter's hospital room was the old Russian. Being physically supported by his nurse, his IV bottle was attached to him along with monitor devices on a stainless-steel pole.

"Do not blame her. It is I who needs to apologize to you, Jacob. My greed caused me to use Anya's love for you. As I stated in my legal paperwork, I was at fault, and I am sorry. Sorry that I used my precious daughter to hurt someone she truly loved, I am sorry," Peter said as he slowly turned, retreating into his room.

Jacob felt emotionally torn between two sides. On one hand, he wanted to believe Anya and Peter, but the memory of his terrifying near-death experience kept resurfacing. Without uttering a word, he locked eyes with Anya, reminiscing about their initial encounter at the company party, their conversations at the farmers market, and their intimacy. He longed to trust Peter's explanation, but it didn't prove easy. If he accepted her father's account, it meant that Peter was responsible for killing Jacob's girlfriend and orchestrating the attempt on his life. On the other hand, if he rejected Peter's version, he would have to believe that Anya was behind everything—a notion he couldn't entirely accept.

"I know you have to go. Can we at least meet again and talk more?" Anya said, nearly begging.

At first, he wanted to shut her down and not give an inch, but his emotional side took hold. He decided there would be no harm in meeting again—somewhere in public, as he knew Stone would want to be close or have others nearby, just in case.

"I imagine that giving you my contact info would be useless, as your father most likely knows where I am staying. Sure, let's talk, but just you and me," Jacob said reluctantly.

"Thank you, Jacob. I appreciate your trust," Anya said with a smile.

"Oh, I don't trust you, Anya, read the room. I want to hear more of what your plans have been," he said, turning to walk away.

"I understand," Anya said.

Jacob stopped and turned back towards her. "That's funny, you never could understand my American sayings, but you understood that one," Jacob said suspiciously, thinking about his reference to reading the room, remembering how Anya would kid him about slang sayings he would say, with her pretending to be confused.

Jacob joined Stone and John as they waited near the elevator. Stone observed his body language closely, considering the unique opportunity to interact with someone who had attempted to take his life. Stone mused that not every lawman gets that chance, realizing that such individuals usually can't provide answers.

"You, ok?" Stone asked.

"Yeah, we need to talk more. I have an idea," Jacob pushed the button to the elevator.

Anya and Peter returned to the hospital room, where the hospital staff helped the feeble old man into his bed. Anya stood beside Peter, holding his hand as he attempted to catch his breath.

"You know what to do," Peter said as his half-open eyes looked into Anya's, his hand slightly squeezing hers.

"Yes, papa. I will take care of it. You get some rest," Anya said, leaving the room as Peter closed his eyes.

"You need to get to the airport. There is a flight to Seoul, and you're on it. I'll brief you on the way," Stone said as they walked out the front door of the hospital. This shocked Jacob. He was not going to work with Stone and would take it on his own. Oh well, he thought, I need to spread my wings sometime.

CHAPTER 10 (Fava)

The Baltiyskiy Proliv "Baltic Strait," a 1200-foot oil tanker hauling thousands of gallons of Russian crude oil, had been sailing nonstop for ten days after leaving the Russian port in Primorsk. It had been clear sailing from the Danish Sea into the Gulf of Finland heading west. In addition to the two dozen crew members from various Baltic countries, one man stood out. Having never worked on an oil tanker, his lack of interest or knowledge was apparent. Nabil Massoudo had one goal in mind: to make his way to the middle of the Atlantic, where he would transfer to another Dark Fleet ship, as it performed a ship-to-ship transfer of illegal oil coming from Russia. The tanker Baltic Strait, a ship owned by Severnaya Energetika, Peter Stanislavski, its Chief Operating Officer, was sailing with the Automatic Identification System shut off, masking the identity of the vessel, hoping to prevent being discovered by U.S. or Allied Navy's watching for Dark Fleet ships that would transfer their illicit oil, sending the crude to other countries willing to take the chance in being added to the sanctions list. Ship-to-ship oil transfers were a dangerous operation. Most of the time, various-sized ships would perform oil transfers to allow smaller ships with shorter drafts to enter a river or harbor; however, the procedure was carried out in calm waters, where the risk of an explosion or spillage was minimized. In the open waters of the Atlantic, where weather can change instantly, these captains risked their crews and ships for large payouts if they weren't killed or caught.

This was of no concern to Nabil, just weeks earlier, when he had escaped what he thought was an assassin team, which had stormed his apartment in Hamburg, Germany, looking for something. He quickly escaped down a rain pipe next to his balcony, breaking his ankle in the descent. Later, he was sent a photo in a compromising position with a young male prostitute he had kindly allowed to stay in his apartment. The sender and his handler wanted to know how he had let himself be placed in such a compromising situation. Nabil was concerned that his value had diminished and his life was in jeopardy.

His laptop, hidden behind a bookshelf at his apartment, contained hundreds of photographs showing items seized by the United States and Allies from Russian oligarchs around the world. The sanctions against Russia for the invasion of Ukraine were meant to weaken Russia's ability to use money the Oligarchs were paying in exchange for the Kremlin's "hands off" policy as the men stripped their country of its wealth. Nabil had learned that a possible attack on Peter Stanislavski was being planned, and he was shadowing the oligarch when someone had attempted to kill Stanislavski by coating a razor with a lethal dose of polonium-210. Nabil was photographing people entering and exiting the hospital Stanislavski had been taken to when Sergey Valenki, Stanislavski's Chief of Security, was killed when starting his car at the hospital. The explosion shell-shocked Nabil as he sat in a Café across the street. He handed his camera to a waiter, believing he could identify the man later and send a team to recover the camera. The last thing Nabil recalls at the café was telling the waiter that the Pretorian would come for the camera.

Fortunately for Nabil, he encoded the SD card files in the camera and laptop with encryption software that would not allow viewing of the photos without the key code. Attempting to view the photos more than three times without the code would corrupt the images, making them unrecoverable. He had received the Orien 37x software from a CIA intelligence officer in Afghanistan when Nabil was living there, helping the United States in photographing al-Qaeda members living in various villages.

Nabil took only one item with him upon his escape from the apartment: a sack, his go bag. He had learned this term from one of his handlers, who had extensive military training.

"You need to have a go bag ready at all times," handler Tom explained to a young, excited Nabil, who knew his handler would make his new life lucrative.

"Why? What would I use this for?" asked Nabil.

"When the shit hits the fan, you won't have time to think about all the things you need to take. So do it in advance. Stash your bag somewhere accessible but not noticeable," Tom said.

Nabil had meticulously gathered small and portable items—essentials to keep him alive until he could find safety. A burner phone, clothes, a Browning .25 caliber handgun known as a Baby Browning, cash, and one additional item—a very dangerous item that he had decided to keep close to him in his locked bag.

"This canister would bring a large amount of money once its contents were disclosed. Just a sample of more to come," he thought to himself.

As Nabil stood outside the ship's control deck, smoking a Cohiba cigar, he let his mind drift. The ocean air was clean and refreshing. The low rumbling sound of the ship's engines gave Nabil a sense of security. The smell of his cigar took him back to a time in Havana, Cuba, where he lived on a 38-foot Islander Sailboat with a young Cuban girl named Isabella. She was a stunning young Cuban woman with captivating features that reflected her mixed heritage. Her dark, almond-shaped eyes always had a spark of curiosity, always seeking new experiences. Her silky, chestnut-brown hair cascaded loosely around her shoulders, framing her radiant and expressive face. Isabella's sun-kissed skin carried a warm glow, highlighting her Cuban roots.

On well-run ships, a crew member would not be allowed to smoke or have open flames on a floating bomb, which is what crew members were frequently reminded they worked on. However, Dark Fleet ships had crew members with less-than-honorable backgrounds. These were men who knew they were violating dozens of international shipping regulations, living on the fringes of making a small fortune or facing prison time for intentionally violating international sanctions. Crews would perform any assignment if the price were right. The ships were less than pristine, with maintenance being performed to get the cargo of crude oil from one point to another. Safety was not a concern, as crews were prepared to abandon their ship in case of a fire or explosion and then claim ignorance about the cargo. Nabil had only one mission. Get to Seoul, South Korea, where he would make his way to Tunnel #4 at the DMZ. A small and undetected tunnel was dug by the North Korean Government, facilitating the exchange of illicit items, one of which Nabil was going to provide to an agent. This item was Nabil's proof that his spymasters could supply much more of the substance, elevating Nabil's credibility.

Tunnel #4 was created after the National Intelligence Service, South Korea's chief intelligence agency, detected the other three tunnels, which were named the "Tunnels of Aggression." Those tunnels had been blocked to prevent North Korean infiltrators from entering South Korea and were now the favorite tourist destination when visiting the country's DMZ region. However, tunnel #4 had been hidden from view by rock cliffs and heavy forest. Only certain people in South Korea knew of their location and would assist Nabil in finding the entrance and avoiding any explosives set to collapse the tunnel if an unsuspecting person chose to enter it without guidance.

"We will reach the transfer location in three hours. Before the oil transfers begin, a rig line from one ship to the other will be used to transfer you over. Have you ever gone zip lining? This is pretty much the same thing," the ship's officer told Nabil.

"Is it dangerous?" Nabil asked ignorantly.

"Everything we do is dangerous. If our cargo off gasses and you have that cigar lit, you can kiss your ass goodbye."

Nabil looked at his Cuban cigar, tossing it overboard.

"Lunch will be served in ten minutes at the Galley," the officer said, turning and entering the ship. Nabil paused a few minutes longer, taking in as much of the sea air as he could and etching the memory in his mind.

Making his way into the Galley, he found several crewmembers standing in line as they carried stainless steel trays to a buffet line. Hot, steaming vegetables and stew were served with warm, fresh-baked rolls and butter. A red gelatin dessert and pudding with whipped cream ended the buffet line. Nabil had skipped breakfast and was feeling his hunger speak to him in the form of a noisy stomach. He made his way to an empty table, grabbing silverware wrapped in a napkin from the bin next to the table.

The stew was good, as Nabil shoveled spoonfuls into his mouth, followed by rolls that had absorbed the stew's juices. He looked around at the other crewmen enjoying their food. The smell of sweat and petroleum mingled with the scent of lunch, filling the air. Nabil felt tired and worn out as it became increasingly hard to catch his breath. Figuring he was reacting to the change from fresh sea air to a smelly room of men, he did not pay much attention to the discomfort. As he continued to eat, he felt worse; his breathing became labored, and he felt lightheaded. He stood and placed his hands on the table, as if he were about to get sick, then he saw it. Sticking out from under a piece of meat in the stew was the round end of a fava bean. Nabil was familiar with the beans. When he was a young boy, his mother would refer to them as the beans of death. Later in life, he learned that he carried a blood disorder referred to as favism. However, the fava bean was one of the oldest crops, dating back nearly 6,000 years; those who were allergic to the bean suffered from acute hemolytic anemia, enlarged spleens, anaphylactic shock, and, on this day, heart failure. Nabil hit the ground like a sack of potatoes, and the other crewmen kept eating without offering assistance. Two men, finishing their lunch and wearing white overalls, slowly picked up their safety helmets, removed their trays from the table, and stepped over the body on the floor. When the men finished placing their dirty trays on a tray holder, they put their hard hats on their heads and approached Nabil's lifeless body. One man propped up the motionless body to obtain a grip under the armpits while the other securely held Nabil's lower legs. They carried him through the ship's hallway to a door leading outside on the upper deck. By the time Nabil's body hit the water, the two men had entered the ship and were walking back to their assignments. The captain of the ship, watching the two men from his chair on the control bridge, removed his Satcomm G63 encrypted phone from his pocket. He typed in several numbers and a text message that read, "No longer an issue." He then pressed the send button to transmit the message. The Satcomm G63 displayed a return message that read, "Received, Pretorian." The captain turned off the Satcomm G63 to prevent anyone from tracking the ship's coordinates.

Two crewmen were instructed to remove Nabil's personal belongings from his lower deck bunk and dispose of them overboard. The Go Bag was hidden under his bunk, and once opened, each man examined the various items, assessed their value, and kept what was important to them. The small, silver, heavy canister without exterior markings was examined. Each man took a turn attempting to open the canister without success. On the wall, a fire axe was mounted for emergencies. The man removed the axe and carefully positioned the canister on the bunk between the rails; with a swift and strong chopping motion, the man struck the canister, causing it to be catapulted upwards, the top coming off and filling the area with a flour-like yellow powder. Both men stepped back and sneezed, waving their hands to clear the air. An examination of the canister did not disclose anything of value. Finding nothing to their interest, the can was gathered with the other property of no value and thrown overboard.

◆ ◆ ◆

13°41'48.7"S by 19°59'29.5"W, nearly in the middle of nowhere on the South Atlantic Ocean, the night skies were open and full of stars; there was no moon visible as this specific night was chosen for no moon illumination. Less light, less detection of two large tanker ships coming dangerously close for an oil transfer. The surface of the water was still, and the only sounds were the low rumble of the ship heading south, flying the flag of Cameroon. There are no running lights, and on this night, oddly enough, there are no lookouts on board. The ship had been on autopilot for eight days. The second ship was ready to receive a load of crude oil in violation of the G7 sanctions, passed weeks prior.

The captain was notified that the Baltic Strait was twenty-eight miles to their port beam and had not yet started reducing its speed. The captain stepped over to the port side of the command deck, raised his binoculars, and scanned for the Baltic Strait. As the ship came into view, he tried to see what activity was visible on board.

"Juan, has the Baltic Strait reduced speed?" the captain asked.

"No sir, still at 15 knots and holding," the officer replied.

Removing the black handset, which resembled an older telephone, from its holder, the captain attempted to hail the Baltic Strait, but there was no response. He wasn't too worried, as ships in the dark fleet maintained radio silence to avoid detection. The radar operator watched his screen, keeping track of the Baltic Strait's position. But then an odd thing happened. A small blip on the radar at the 4 o'clock position came on momentarily and went off.

"Captain, I have a contact at one zero, 30 miles out. But now it's gone," he said, looking at the captain inquisitively.

The captain turned his attention to the radar as he and the sailor watched for the return of the contact signal. Attention was now turned to the starboard side of the ship as the captain attempted to ascertain if the signal was a ship in transit or a military ship approaching to investigate why two tankers were meeting without their automatic identification systems active.

The captain returned to the Baltic Strait, which had still not slowed and was now behind the ship, turning and approaching. The captain noted that the Baltic Strait was listing starboard as it made its turn.

"Keep trying to raise them on the radio; find out why they are approaching our location so fast. All ahead, one half. We're a sitting duck," the captain's voice now taking on a tone of concern.

The ship's engines began to spin, but it's not easy to bring a ship of that size and weight to a quick speed from a near stop. Yet the Baltic Strait continued to bear down on its sister ship, the Orion Arrow. The captain could not see anyone on the bridge or workers on the deck. Something was wrong as the Baltic Strait advanced at full speed, coming to a direct matching course of the Orion Arrow. Panic broke out on the deck as crewmen prepared for what they never thought could happen. Collision horns were blaring as the captain yelled into his microphone in hopes of getting the attention on the bridge of the Baltic Strait. By the time they realized they were being overtaken, it was too late.

On the second floor of the Volcano Pub at Cat Hill, St. Helena on Ascension Island, locals enjoyed watching the stars out over the water. Robert enjoyed some lasagna and a garlic roll with a rum and Coke. The night was pitch black, with a show of stars above. The sound of waves in the distance became another part of the ambiance of this beautiful Island that Robert had called home for the last two years.

As the mushroom cloud of bright orange lit the ocean, everyone went silent, their attention turning to the sea, watching until the light of the two burning ships vanished into the darkness. On such a small Island, there wasn't much they could do except watch and wonder.

CHAPTER 11 (Seoul)

Trying to sleep on a 14-hour flight was nearly impossible. Even though Jacob was in Premium Class on Air Premia, the constant seatbelt sign going on and off, with the flight attendants announcing in Korean and then switching to English to follow the overhead signs, could cause a person to experience continuous sleep deprivation. Even though flight attendants electronically darkened the windows, keeping out the sun, Jacob tossed and turned. He would close his eyes and wander off to a time when his chartered plane would fly him and Anya to their destinations. The food and the king-sized bed were what he needed. And just for a moment, a fleeting moment, he could recall Anya's perfume and the softness of her body, as she would lie across him naked, her face next to his, in a deep sleep. DING.

"Ladies and Gentlemen, the Captain has turned on the seat belt sign. Please be sure your seat belts are fastened and refrain from using the lavatories."

Awake again. He could feel the fatigue in his eyelids as he stared at the LCD screen on the seat in front of him, slowly ticking away at the miles left to fly.

He turned his focus to the mission at hand. Seoul, South Korea. He was trying to locate a tunnel that had been a story for years, a legend of the South Koreans. In the files taken from Nabil's laptop, there were longitude and latitude references directly at the Demilitarized Zone, also referred to as the DMZ. Jacob planned to visit Tunnel 2 at the DMZ, taking a local tour bus. Once there, he would "accidentally" wander from the group. Locating the Tunnel would explain why Nabil and his handler were interested in it. He just needed to stay out of sight of the U.S. and South Korean Military that routinely searched the DMZ for defectors trying to cross. And, of course, not get shot by some young North Korean Soldier who wanted to make points by taking out what he thought was one of their defectors by accident. And let's not forget about the Improvised Explosive Devices (IED) that the tunnel was most likely booby-trapped with to stop unwelcome visitors.

Jacob figured that if he successfully located the tunnel, he could alert the Joint Forces Command in Seoul, which could dispatch explosives experts to clear the entrance. But only if he could do this discreetly so as not to tip off the North Koreans, who were suspected of helping Russia.

To help speed things along, a local tour guide and fixer used by the U.S. Embassy, Jay Kim, would pick up Jacob at the Incheon airport when he landed and cleared customs. Although Jacob did not carry any law enforcement credentials, his passport was equipped with an embedded tracking and identification chip the size of a hair under his photo. This chip alerted the Customs Agent not to question Jacob but to let him move on.

Jacob dozed off again, only to be awakened by the meal service attendants coming down the aisle. The flight attendant served him a traditional Korean meal in elegant triangle dishes. Having never tried Bibimbap, Jacob unwrapped the foil liner to be immediately overcome by the wonderful smell of warm rice topped with vegetables, beef, and a small tube of an unknown sauce. After a few bites, he was sold and decided to squeeze out the thick red paste from the tube. Taking a forkful of vegetables and a healthy paste sample, he quickly found out what it was: red chili pepper paste. The coughing was uncontrollable. The flight attendant recognized the distress, bringing Jacob a large bottle of water to put out the fire in his mouth. His nose ran, and his eyes teared. He had attended Texas chili cookoffs where the samples were cooked with ghost peppers and Carolina Reapers, which rated over one million on the Scoville Scale, a way of registering pepper heat. This paste was up there with the best of them, he thought as he tried to control the pain in his mouth and sinuses.

After this food encounter, Jacob could hardly eat the dessert and sat recovering as the final hours of the flight approached. Landing at Incheon International Airport in a 787 Dreamliner was like no other landing Jacob could recall. His window was still greyed out when the plane touched down, and he could not feel the plane on the runway until the pilot engaged the reverse thrust. The force made Jacob glad he was seat-belted in, with the sounds of items hitting the floor around him.

His departure from the plane was quick as he was flying Premium Economy. Up the ramp and to the luggage carousel, where his suitcase was the second one in line. Things clicked and moved briskly when two customs officers, accompanied by a dog on a leash, approached him.

"How was your flight, Sir?" One man asked in perfect English as his dog, wagging his tail, quickly walked about the suitcase, sniffing each side.

"Excellent. Long but very nice," trying not to look unusual.

"Very good, and what is the reason for visiting?" The other man asked with a slight smile on his face.

Jacob recited the lines he had memorized and practiced on the flight as only Cassius and Assistant Director Bennet knew why he was there.

"Oh, to see Seoul, visit the places, and try the food. Some of which I just got a taste of on the plane. That red paste was a killer," he said, making a pained face.

Both officers chuckled at the comment, fully aware of what Jacob was alluding to. "Ah, yes, Gochujang will catch you every time. Enjoy your stay." And with that, they were off to inspect other luggage.

A few more stops for passport verification and finger scanning, a standard procedure in this time of heightened security.

Jacob walked out of door number two, where the crowds waited for the tiered travelers and their families. Scanning the drivers holding professionally printed signs, he wasn't quite sure what he was looking for. Since he had never met Jay, it was anyone's guess if he was even in the crowd. Jacob slowly moved through the gathering until a young man dressed in a Stanford University sweatshirt stepped forward, his gaze fixed on Jacob.

"Jay Kim," as he patted his chest. "You are Jacob?" he asked with a smile.

"Yes, Jacob Westerly." He reached out to shake the man's hand, but the man quickly grabbed Jacob's carry-on and turned.

"Follow me, I will take you to the car," he said, walking off in almost a sprint. Jacob quickly followed behind with his other luggage, trying to navigate the carpeted floors.

"I was told I should get a wi-fi egg while I was here. Do you know where I can get one of those?" Jacob asked Jay as he tried to keep up with his pace.

"Don't need," was the response.

Jacob followed his driver's instructions, unsure of what else to do. Jay's KIA van was parked outside the exit door with the engine running. He took out his remote control, unlocked the van, and lifted the back door.

"You ride next to me," Jay said in his heavy Korean accent, pointing towards the front of the van as he loaded the luggage into the back compartment. Jacob settled into the front passenger's seat, noticing the spacious interior and the large screen positioned in the middle of the dashboard, slightly angled toward the driver.

Jay made his way to the driver's seat, and in a flash, they were speeding off out of the airport's kayos. Jacob was observing Jay's multitasking ability, but when he took his hands off the wheel, intently staring at his phone screen, Jacob nearly reached over to grab the wheel out of panic. But then Jacob noticed something. The van was driving itself. Even as they approached an exit, the van would signal and slowly move over lanes while slowing. It then took the turn with Jay occasionally looking up like a proud parent checking his child's driving performance.

"It can drive itself," looking at Jacob with a smile.

Jacob's attention was firmly fixed out the front window as he concentrated on the traffic around them—traffic that had real drivers actually steering their cars. One thing that impressed him about Korean highways was that everyone was adhering to the speed limit. Unlike in the United States, where it always seemed like a race with everyone jockeying for position, the traffic was very orderly here.

"Everyone is doing the speed limit," Jacob remarked.

Jay looked up, scanning the horizon, and then pointed ahead.

"There. You see those lights? Police speed cameras. If I speed, I get a ticket in the mail," he said, looking back at his cell phone screen.

"How far is my hotel from here?" Jacob asked.

"About, uh, one hour," he said, pointing to his GPS display.

Jacob leaned back and took in the scenery as the self-driving van moved forward. A light dusting of snow began to fall. His thoughts drifted back to his old apartment in San Francisco and his Maine Coon cat, Tola. There was a time, just before his girlfriend Lisa had been murdered in front of the Ferry Building, when he and Lisa treated Tola as if she were their child, spoiling her at dinner and buying her Christmas gifts. He missed those days. For a moment, he wondered how Anya was doing, where she was, and how she was spending her time. He couldn't help but think of the good times, but then the memories of all the bad moments with Anya came rushing back to fill his thoughts.

He had closed his eyes, lulled by the gentle sway of the car. However, these thoughts quickly roused him as he took a deep breath and sat up in the seat. Jay noticed Jacob's movement and glanced over at him.

"Who is Anya? You kept saying that name with eyes closed. A lover?" He smiled.

"A chapter of my life I've closed," he said as he looked out the window.

As they pulled up to the Marriott's Courtyard, Jacob gathered his shoulder bag and moved to the back of Jay's van to retrieve his other bag. However, Jay had placed it on the ground, shut the hatchback, and was guiding Jacob towards the large turnstile doors to enter the hotel.

Wow, this guy is working for his tip, Jacob thought, as Jay walked directly past the concierge desk, where two young men smiled and watched the two men pass by, not offering assistance to a guest who seemed to know the routine. Jay stopped at the guest elevators that led them to the first-floor check-in desk.

"Thank you. I can take it from here," Jacob said with a smile, reaching for his bag.

"No problem, I was told to take care of you and keep you safe," Jay said, looking directly at Jacob.

"Keep me safe? Why would I not be safe in Seoul?" He tried to maintain the façade of a businessman on the go. After all, he knew that the department had hired Jay, but Jacob wasn't sure how much this guy knew about Jacob's visit to Korea.

"I was told to get you to your room," Jay explained as they exited the elevator, stepping back while Jacob checked in.

The elevator ride to the 18th floor was brief as the two men stepped out and proceeded to room 1825. With a quick swipe of the key at the door, they entered a well-laid-out room. The lights were off, and after turning them on, Jay motioned to Jacob for his room key. Jay pointed to the small plastic holder on the wall and inserted the key.

"If you do not put the key in the holder, the lights go out after 5 minutes," Jay explained.

"Yes, of course," Jacob said, trying not to look ignorant.

Jacob looked out the window and was impressed by the view of Seoul Tower on the hill and the bustling marketplace across the street. To the right of the market, he could see the ancient gates of the city. Tourists were everywhere, and buses lined the roads in a choreographed routine of stopping and starting that Jacob found familiar in any big city he had visited.

He paused as he turned toward Jay, a moment of panic putting him on high alert. Jay held a small automatic handgun in his right hand, loading a full clip of ammunition into the bottom of the gun. Jacob had his duty weapon with him, but it was locked in a gun box in his checked luggage on the bed. He had no time to retrieve it and quickly scanned the room for anything he could turn into a weapon. There on the counter, next to several wine glasses and a bottle of complimentary wine left by the hotel, was a long corkscrew with a wooden handle. He thought about creating a distraction while grabbing the corkscrew and aiming for Jay's eye. This should divert him long enough for Jacob to retrieve his weapon and fire a shot while his adversary struggles with the eye injury. Just as he reached for the corkscrew, Jay placed the gun on the bed.

"I was told to make sure you had a backup gun," Jay said as he laid two additional ammo clips next to the gun. Jacob shifted from red to yellow alert. However, his adrenaline hadn't received the memo from his brain, so Jacob took a deep breath, trying to keep his body appearing relaxed.

"Good idea," Jacob said as calmly as he could manage in a state of adrenaline overload.

Jay stood smiling and looked down at Jacob's hand holding the cork remover, and smiled.

"No drinks for me, too early. I have a long drive back," Jay turned and walked towards the door. He paused and placed a business card containing the door key in the wall holder.

"You call if you need me, okay, Jacob?" The door closed without giving Jacob a chance to respond.

Jacob dropped into the chair next to the window table and took a long breath.

"Holy shit," he said, looking out the window.

Confirming the door was locked, Jacob removed a small electronic box with a slightly bent antenna. When he turned the knob, a pulsing light flashed with a high-pitched sound until he adjusted it, and the lights went out, along with the noise. With a methodically slow movement, Jacob moved the device over smoke detectors, televisions, and the phone. No noise, no lights, the room was clear of internally placed microphones and cameras. However, this did not eliminate the phone on the dresser next to the bed. He could unplug it. However, a smart intelligence service would equip the phone with an independent microphone, allowing it to monitor the room even when unplugged. Jacob had learned in training that no hotel room was considered secure. A hotel room was an open source for listening devices, such as those from cameras or microphones installed in the finished walls. His best option was always to assume he was being listened to in the room and use his scrambled cell phone for any communication outside the hotel.

The department's phone was always set up to track him, and as a backup, he wore a small, stick-on device on the back of his arm that functioned as both a continuous glucose health monitor and a satellite tracking device.

He picked up the phone and dialed the concierge on the first floor.

"Good afternoon, this is Jacob Westerly in 1825. Can you book me a seat on a tour to the DMZ for tomorrow?"

"One moment Mr. Westerly, let me check on that," the phone went silent for 20 seconds before another voice answered.

"Good afternoon, Mr. Westerly. I understand you wish to tour the DMZ. Is there a specific tunnel among the three you are interested in?"

"Oh my, I hadn't done much research. However, I understand there is one that has an observation deck with viewing glasses," he said, sounding uninformed.

"Yes, tunnel two. The tour also includes lunch and will pick you up in front of the hotel at 8 a.m. Does that work for you?" she asked.

"Yes, perfect. Can you charge that to my room?"

"Of course, Mr. Westerly. Enjoy your tour," the call ended.

Jacob spent an hour on his laptop studying Tunnel 2's area on Google Earth. He could see the location where the tour buses would arrive. He thought about his plan to walk away while taking photos, and when the time came, he would travel down the road with his mapping app indicating his arrival at the longitude and latitude. This information had not been confirmed, and upon viewing the satellite images, the parking lot for the buses appeared to have a walking path leading toward the long/lat coordinates; however, no accurate details existed due to the dense forest cover. Time for some food.

Walking out of the Marriott Courtyard, Jacob could smell the assortment of flavors wafting from across the street at the Namdaemum Vegetable Hotteok. He was unfamiliar with the deep-fried stuffed bread offered at a street kiosk; however, standing in line with a dozen other people ultimately paid off. The bread he chose was hot, steaming, and flavored with cinnamon and brown sugar. Jacob strolled through the open-air market while enjoying his Hotteok, which he later learned was a sweet Korean pancake.

Walking along the vendors' kiosks, his eye caught a full-length garment hanging in the window, with a sign that read "Hanbok Inside." He stepped inside the shop and found that he was all alone.

"Hello?" Jacob announced, looking past dozens of garments stuffed on hanging racks.

An older, very short woman stepped out and greeted him in Korean. She made a statement while pulling out a Hanbok, doing her best to explain the garment to the clueless American standing in front of her.

"I'm sorry, I don't speak Korean, do you speak English?" he asked, with doubts.

The woman nodded affirmatively, and Jacob decided to ask more.

"These look fantastic. Are they for men, women, or both?" Touching the one hanging in the window.

The woman seemed impressed with Jacob's selection and used a stick with a hook to reach up and take the garment from the window. Jacob examined it and was intrigued by the fine stitches and cloth.

Even as a young man in the Bay Area, Jacob was interested in fine clothing. Unfortunately, as a coder in a 20-something firm, he never found the reason to own good clothing. His fiancée Lisa would occasionally buy him a nice Jimmy Buffett or Tommy Bahama shirt; however, his main dress style was limited to T-shirts and baggy pants. But something caught his eye with this garment. He had no idea where he would wear it, except maybe the Chuseok Festival in San Francisco, if he returned. He and Lisa would attend every year, sitting on the lawn of the Presidio Parade Ground, eating traditional food of Korea, and watching hours of entertainment on stage. His mind drifted as he looked at the Hanbok. A voice spoke to him, not the sales clerk but a British voice.

"You would look good in that at a sales meeting," came from the open door.

Jacob turned and was speechless.

"Olivia Hawthorne? What are you doing here?" Recalling the last time he saw the beautiful red-haired MI6 agent was when he had dinner with her, Stone, and Agent Hamish at the Gatehouse Pub.

"The Distillery sent me to research different liquors of this country," smiling with an apparent intent of only the two of them knowing what the distillery meant.

"Are you staying nearby? How long are you here for?" Jacob's questions seemed to trip over the previous one.

The saleswoman, realizing that the beautiful red-headed woman was more appealing to her customer than the Hanbok, let out a sigh and turned to hang the Hanbok back in its original place.

"Yes, I'm staying at Fraser Place, just around the corner from your hotel,"

Jacob paused. Everything went quiet as he focused on Olivia's last statement. How did she know he was at the Marriott's Courtyard, which was, in fact, just around the corner from Fraser Place?

"Let's walk," Jacob said as the two agents left the shop and stepped into a quiet opening.

"I never said where I was staying," Jacob said, standing face-to-face with Olivia.

He could smell her perfume, the same as she wore the night they met at the Pub. Her green eyes again, memorizing Jacob. His mind drifted. She reached out, taking his hand. Jacob felt as if he had been paralyzed and could not move. His breath slowed as he waited for Olivia to answer.

"We are both here for the same reason," she paused. Several reasons flashed through his mind, none of which were mission-related.

"Ah, yes, for products that our distilleries are interested in," He smiled as Olivia gently squeezed his hand, releasing it.

"I am starving, how about you? I know of a wonderful little Korean Vegan restaurant just off the beaten track," she turned to walk off before Jacob could answer. He followed, trying to keep up while avoiding the tourists.

After nearly a mile, they arrived at a busy yet small alley in the Jongno District. Cars were passing by within inches, and Jacob was getting concerned about being an obvious tourist walking down an alley; however, Olivia appeared to be comfortable with her surroundings.

"Here we go," Olivia said, opening a wooden door with the name VEGAN INSTA above. They walked through a quiet, enclosed courtyard and entered the counter to order.

"What looks good?" she asked as they stared at the menu.

"Uh, I'm not sure, as I have never had Korean Vegan before," Jacob said in a low and slow voice while he scanned the menu.

The man behind the counter said a few words to Olivia in Korean, who smiled and answered in Korean. Jacob was impressed with her proficiency in foreign languages.

"That Kimchi Quesadilla looks good. And I guess you can't go wrong in Korea with a California roll,"

Olivia looked at Jacob and smiled. "The man knows what he likes," she exclaimed.

Olivia ordered the Curry Fried Soy Chicken and an order of Fried Dumplings. The man entered the prices into the register as Jacob stepped forward, credit card in hand.

"Put your money away. It's no good here," Olive said, handing her credit card to the cashier.

They selected a private room next to the entry doors with a sliding glass door, privacy, and a good view of people eating and entering the restaurant. As they sat, Jacob sipped his water and looked at Olivia. He remembered his last meeting with her and how beautiful she looked then. Things had not changed; he was still captivated by her green eyes and auburn hair pulled back into a ponytail.

"So, is it just coincidence we met here in Seoul? Of all the gin joints in all the towns in all the world, Olivia walks into mine," Jacob tried his best Humphrey Bogart imitation.

Olivia paused, checking her phone, and looked over the top of her reading glasses. A smile came over her face.

"James Cagney?" she said.

Jacob dropped his head and shook it slightly. He slowly raised his head, smiling with a slight giggle.

"Casablanca? Bogart?"

"Oh yes, the other American gangster," she said sarcastically.

"Bogie wasn't a…" she interrupted him by raising her hand in a gesture to stop.

"When are you heading to the tunnel?" she asked

Jacob paused and thought about whether it was a good idea to show all his cards at once. After all, why was Olivia here, in the same town, next to the same hotel where he was staying? What was her end game in all of this?

"Tunnel? Not sure what you mean?" he said, testing the water.

She sighed. "You know exactly what I mean. Tunnel 4. Look, Jacob, I understand you are cautious about disclosing your mission; I get it. But our time is limited, and our intel says that whatever is in that tunnel is about to be moved. Once it's gone, we'll be chasing our tails, trying to play catch-up. So, let's just work together and get this done quickly, ok?" Staring directly into Jacobs's eyes, realizing the man across from her was mesmerized.

Jacob held her gaze, searching for signs of a lie—and finding none. Just the quiet intensity he remembered from that night at the Gatehouse Pub, when secrets danced between them and danger felt almost romantic.

Their food sat untouched.

"Jacob," Olivia said softly, "we don't have time to pretend we're not on the same side."

He let out a slow breath, his resistance unraveling under the weight of her voice, her eyes, the way she leaned toward him like she already knew the choice he'd make.

"I don't like surprises," he murmured.

"Then you're going to hate the next forty-eight hours," she replied with a half-smile, brushing a loose strand of hair behind her ear.

Jacob reached across the table, fingers grazing hers—not quite a touch, more a question than an answer.

She met him halfway.

Her hand was warm. Familiar. Dangerous.

For a moment, the noise outside disappeared. The world was reduced to the soft clink of glasses, the pulse of adrenaline, and the shared weight of something neither of them would name.

"So," she whispered, "do we have a truce?"

Jacob gave the faintest nod, their fingers still linked.

The room felt warmer now, or maybe it was just her.

Then Olivia glanced toward the frosted glass of the booth door. Her expression shifted.

She pulled her hand back.

"We're being watched," she said, barely moving her lips. "Don't look. Just smile like I told a good joke."

Jacob's smile flickered into place, but his heart thudded harder.

Of course, they were being watched.

It was never just lunch.

The city had quieted under a blanket of misty rain, the streets shimmering under scattered pools of neon. Jacob and Olivia walked in silence, their footsteps soft on the wet pavement as they made their way through back alleys and side streets. No tail, no eyes — at least none Jacob could spot.

They reached the Marriott's Courtyard just as the drizzle turned to a steadier fall. Olivia didn't wait for an invitation; she simply followed him through the glass doors, past the dim-lit lobby, and into the elevator. Neither spoke. But the silence between them was thick with everything they weren't saying.

On the 18th floor, Jacob opened the door to his room and stepped aside. She walked in without hesitation, pausing in the center of the room as though deciding whether she was staying for a moment or the night.

Then she turned.

He moved toward her, not rushed, not tentative. Just certain. Their lips met in a slow, deep kiss, the kind that stripped away pretense. She pressed against him, pulling him toward the bed, and this time, he didn't hold back.

They undressed between kisses and glances, with the soft rustle of fabric hitting the floor and the hum of rain outside as their only soundtrack. Her skin was warm beneath his hands; his touch was careful, then urgent, then careful again. She traced the scar on his shoulder with her fingers. He buried his face in her neck like a man remembering something he hadn't realized he'd forgotten.

When they finally collapsed together, tangled in the sheets, breathless and quiet, Olivia's head rested on his chest, rising and falling with each slow breath.

Neither of them spoke.

Jacob felt her fingertips slide gently across his ribs, absently, like she was grounding herself in something real.

Within minutes, her breathing slowed. She was asleep.

Jacob stayed awake a little longer, watching the ceiling, one arm wrapped around her. There were still too many questions. About the tunnel. About her being in Seoul. About what she wanted — and what she already knew.

But for now, in this quiet room above a city full of secrets, those questions could wait.

He closed his eyes and let himself drift, Olivia's warmth beside him, the rain still whispering against the window.

The hotel phone rang several times before Jacob stirred himself awake.

"Hello?" Jacob tried to sound awake but had a hard time pretending.

"Yes, Mr. Westerly, this is the front desk. We are informing all guests that President Yoon Suk Yeol has declared a state of emergency and martial law. Your tour bus will arrive at 8 a.m. outside the hotel lobby. However, I am not sure if they will be allowed to pick you up. We will keep you updated," as the phone hung up. Moments later, Jacobs' phone lit up with alerts from the U.S. Embassy in Seoul, warning of martial law but providing no specific details other than to avoid large crowds or protests.

Jacob fought the urge to crawl back into bed for what he told himself would be a ten-minute nap, but he knew it would turn into several hours. There was nothing he could do about the martial law, he figured, so he might as well get on the tour bus and leave Seoul behind.

The room was still dark, but the rising sun had begun to bathe the hills and the Seoul Tower in a soft, golden light. Jacob pulled back the drapes and looked down at the streets below. Two military vehicles and about a dozen soldiers stood around a tank idling in the middle of the road, as if waiting for orders. Yet below his 18th-story window, buses and commuters moved through the streets, seemingly unfazed by the military presence.

Seoul was waking up.

The bathroom light cast a soft glow, and through the frosted glass separating the shower from the sleeping area, the silhouette of a perfectly shaped, nude figure was visible. Olivia had woken earlier and decided to shower and change into the clothes she'd purchased the day before, just as Jacob had caught sight of her.

"Hey there, sailor. What brings you to town?" Olivia teased, standing in nothing but a towel, a playful glint in her eye.

Jacob grinned, reclining with his hands behind his head as he watched her dry off. "Oh, just thought I'd enjoy the military parade outside while we wait to see if our mission gets scrubbed."

"What? Are you serious?" she said, her tone shifting as she hurried to the window. She pulled back the curtain and stared down, taking in the unexpected sight below.

Olivia quickly dressed and drank a cup of coffee that Jacob had made from the room coffee machine. Standing at the window and watching the military as she sipped her coffee. Then, unexpectedly, she placed her cup on the windowsill and grabbed her coat.

"Come on, the bus just arrived, and the soldiers have driven off. Let's see if we can move forward," walking towards the door.

"Wait a minute," Jacob said, worry creeping into his voice. "Even if we make it to the bus, who knows what we'll run into along the way—roadblocks, militias, angry anti-American crowds?"

"We can't sit around waiting for someone to tell us what to do," Olivia said firmly. "We have to keep moving forward. You can stay here if you want, but I'm going." She turned toward the door.

"Ah, shit—okay, okay, I'm with you," Jacob said, throwing up his hands. "Not that I think anyone's going to target me for being American. I just know how the world feels about you Brits."

Olivia turned back with a sarcastic smile. "Charming as ever."

Jacob and Olivia grabbed a quick coffee and Danish at the café downstairs before walking outside to meet the tour bus, which was picking them up for a tour of the DMZ tunnels. The bus driver did not indicate any issues and permitted the two agents on board. On the bus, neither spoke. They knew the plan was to blend in with the crowd at the final destination and then hike into the wooded area, searching for the coordinates that led to the tunnel.

The conversation among passengers from all over the world centered on the declaration of martial law. Some Koreans expressed concern that they did not want South Korea to go back to the old days when martial law was frequently invoked and rights curtailed.

Once they arrived, the tour guides emphasized that the tourists must stay together. Losing the crowd was easy. However, locating the coordinates on Jacob's GPS app quickly led them to hike through a near-jungle environment.

"This is going to take hours," Jacob said.

"That's okay," Olivia replied in a low voice, ducking under branches and swatting away insects. "The tour team will alert the authorities—my people have already briefed them—and the bus will return without us."

Jacob checked his GPS. Target coordinates 38.305864, 127.295932.

"Just over that ridge. There should be a slight clearing." Jacob said, pointing to a slight hill.

Without warning, Olivia yanked him to the ground. They lay still, breathing heavily, as a military truck rumbled past in the opposite direction.

"Thanks," Jacob whispered, Olivia's body still pressed against his, her breath quick and shallow. For a moment, neither moved, caught in the stillness.

"That was way too close," she snapped. "Start paying attention to the sounds around you—your lack of awareness could get us both killed."

"Yes, ma'am," he said, still a bit rattled. Then, straightening up with exaggerated stiffness, he added, "Right this way, ma'am," and began marching ahead with comically rigid arms, mimicking a British soldier on parade.

"You know, I could kick your ass if needed," she snipped back.

"Understood, ma'am," he said, delivering his best attempt at a British flat-handed salute—somewhere between royal guard and awkward tourist—before spinning on his heel with dramatic flair and continuing on.

As the two agents came to the crest of the hill, they both crouched down, stopping and watching. Jacob removed a small pair of binoculars from his backpack, focusing in on a truck several hundred yards ahead of their position.

Three figures stood around what looked like an unremarkable patch of forest. But Jacob's trained eye caught the metal sheen through the brush. A door—massive, rusted, and wrong. Two of the men were Korean, plainclothes, but exuding military discipline. The third, a pale European with the build of a former Spetsnaz operative, barked orders in fluent Russian.

They secured the door with a lock-box and camouflage netting. Minutes later, the men vanished into the woods.

Jacob and Olivia moved in.

Using a pair of advanced NATO-grade magnetic decoders, Olivia worked the lock while Jacob kept watch, his sidearm concealed but ready. A soft click echoed through the brush. The door creaked open, revealing a black maw of earth and rust.

They entered.

Downward, they carefully walked. The tunnel was wide enough for a military truck, the walls reinforced with North Korean steel plating. At intervals, flickering emergency lights cast long shadows. The air smelled of ozone, decay, and something worse—radiation, faint but unmistakable.

Hours passed.

Then, a thunderous clang echoed behind them—the door.

Locked.

Jacob tried the comms. Dead. Either the tunnel blocked the signal, or they were being jammed.

"No choice now," Olivia said, voice cold and sharp. "We keep going."

Deep inside the bowels of the tunnel, they found it.

A sealed chamber, lead-lined, with warning signs in Cyrillic, Korean, and Arabic. The plutonium was encased in military-grade containers, six of them. Enough to level half a city. Olivia carefully extracted a sample into a containment canister, the device humming softly as it calibrated and sealed.

They moved on, hoping for a secondary exit—and found one.

A narrow shaft, camouflaged from the outside, led them to a forest clearing far beyond the DMZ's southern line.

But they were in the North now.

They moved fast, low, avoiding thermal sensors and patrols, navigating by satellite coordinates and instinct. The DMZ loomed ahead, guarded by concrete walls and watchtowers.

Almost across.

"Meomchow! An geuleomyeon ssol geoya," a voice roared behind them.

Three North Korean soldiers emerged from the brush, rifles raised, faces drawn with fury and fear. Jacob froze, his hand twitching near his pistol. Their command was to stop, or they would shoot.

"Don't," Olivia warned under her breath.

The standoff began, tension vibrating in the frozen air like a live wire.

Then, a shout from the south.

American and South Korean troops emerged, weapons drawn, fingers on triggers. One false move and the demilitarized zone would erupt into a shooting gallery.

"Hold your fire!" came a voice from a U.S. officer. "They're ours!"

The North Koreans hesitated.

Then Olivia stepped forward.

Slowly, deliberately, she raised the canister above her head. Her voice rang clear, cool, and lethal.

"If you shoot me, I drop this. Radiation will flood this area. You'll never go home. You'll never see your families again. You'll die slowly, in agony," her words directed to the North Korean Soldiers who must have understood English, looking at each other for direction.

Silence.

Jacob counted three heartbeats. Four.

Then, a barked order came from behind the North Koreans—their commander. Reluctantly, the soldiers lowered their weapons.

Jacob and Olivia stepped across the line. Hands were on them in moments—American uniforms, shouting over radios. The canister was taken and loaded into a radiation-safe case. A CIA official with a stern face and darker intentions greeted them with a nod.

"You're coming with me," he said.

Olivia looked to Jacob.

He gave a half-smile. "Another day in paradise."

As helicopters arrived overhead and the sun broke over the jagged border, the two agents disappeared into the waiting vehicles—two shadows retreating from the edge of war, carrying proof of a threat no one else had dared to find.

Jacob caught a glimpse from his helicopter as they passed by the entrance point to the hidden tunnel. Large military trucks with personnel dressed in Haz-mat suits were slowly entering the rusty door.

The CIA officer tapped Jacob on the shoulder.

"Agent Westerly, I have orders to put you on the next commercial flight out of Seoul to Italy. You'll receive a briefing packet when we get to the airport," looking back as if he was pleased that these two agents would be out of his hair.

Olivia placed her hand on Jacob's knee and leaned close.

"I guess I'll see you on our next vacation," she said with a slight smile on her face.

CHAPTER 12 (Forte del Marmi)

The twelve-hour flight from Seoul to Forte del Marmi, Italy, provided Jacob time to nap, eat, and review the documents Stone had provided. The Airbus A320, operated under the Air France title, lifted off the runway with its Pratt & Whitney GTF engines making barely a sound.

Assistant Director Bennet contacted Stone the night before, providing information from Interpol's Financial Crime and Anti-Corruption Center (IFCACC). The IFCACC had been collaborating with the Ukrainian Asset and Recovery Management Agency (ARMA) when they discovered a document found during a raid of a home owned by a Russian oligarch in Forte del Marmi. In their interview with the Russian, they learned that the document was a land grant from Mussolini to Hitler before World War II began. A photograph of Hitler and Mussolini laughing together in a convertible car hung on the wall of the oligarch's office, supporting the claim of the document's authenticity. However, something about the document's appearance seemed off, and IFCACC agents could not identify the issue. The document had never been seen before, which significantly increased its value to millions of dollars. Bennet offered to send an agent to examine the document on-site, and they accepted. Jacob felt somewhat out of place being sent alone while Stone stayed behind to work on Nabil's files on his laptop. He figured he needed to gain experience eventually, without Stone overseeing his every move, and the past 48 hours in Seoul had demonstrated his ability to take charge and get the job done. Document identification was Jacob's area of expertise at FLETC. He felt confident examining the document and knew the proper identification steps to follow.

The aircraft landed in Florence, and Jacob quickly transferred to a waiting helicopter operated by BLADE Urban Air Mobility. The Airbus H-155 powered up with the blades rotating quickly. Jacob was familiar with helicopter flight as his yacht previously housed an Airbus 130, Aston Martin Edition helicopter that would fly him and Anya to Maui for their pre-wedding plans. A marriage that was annulled after her attempt on his life. Jacob sat quietly as the helicopter lifted off the ground, remembering when he first flew with Anya on their helicopter en route to his ship, the Anastasia Dream. He felt comfortable with that period.

As the helicopter approached the Hotel Principe from the Ligurian Sea side of the hotel, Jacob noticed the setting sun glistening off the beautiful white structure with outdoor seating on the fourth-floor restaurant. A blue crystal-clear pool was located feet from the back of the building, and people were sipping cocktails and watching the sunset. Several took notice of the approaching helicopter, pausing their meal to see if the passenger was a celebrity or political figure who frequented the establishment.

Jacob approached the check-in desk, surveying the area around him as he had been trained to do, noting people sitting alone who might be paying more attention to his arrival than normal. He placed his black titanium American Express card on the counter as he adjusted his sunglasses to the top of his head.

"Mr. Westerly, it is an honor to have you with us. Your suite is ready," the clerk said, handing Jacob his credit card and room keycard. "A message has arrived for you," handing Jacob a small envelope containing a folded paper. On the paper, a note was handwritten, with the number 414 written in ink.

"Any idea who left this?" Jacob asked.

"No sir, it was here an hour ago when I arrived for work. The stationary is from this hotel," the clerk pointed out.

"Can you please tell me who is in room 414?"

"No sir, I cannot. Hotel policy prevents it," the clerk said politely.

Jacob removed his badge wallet, opened it, and placed it in front of the clerk.

"Very beautiful, the detail is impressive, and in America, this might get you answers, but not here, sorry," the clerk smiled, unimpressed with the lawman's credentials.

Jacob folded his badge wallet, placing it in his upper suit coat pocket. Removing a five Euro note, he placed it on the desk in front of the desk clerk who was typing into the computer. He glanced over and returned his attention to the screen. He picked up the Euro and placed it back on the elevated counter between him and Jacob.

"I'm sorry sir but you must have dropped this five-dollar Euro, five U.S. dollars with change," looking at Jacob with an annoyed glaze.

Jacob removed another bill from his pocket, placing it in front of the clerk. The clerk casually looked at the U.S. one-hundred-dollar note and immediately stopped typing, paying close attention to the man before him.

"Yes, sir, I believe the guest in room 414 is registered as Anastasia Lenkov," he said as the U.S. bill quickly slipped into his pants pocket.

Jacob stood there stunned. She was here. Did she know I would be, he thought? Then, like a dream, he could smell her Gardenia perfume as it swirled around him. How was this possible? Jacob noticed the desk clerk looking beyond him as if preparing to greet another guest.

"I thought you might recognize the name," a voice came from directly behind him.

His turn placed him within a couple of feet of Anya, who was wearing a large-brimmed sunhat and Cartier dark square sunglasses. Her Versace Medusa one-piece swimsuit and wrap, worn with Gucci leather Espadrille high-heel shoes, gave her the essence of a beautiful woman who enjoyed being outside the pool for show only.

"Of all the Gin joints in all the towns, you show up here," Jacob said sarcastically, again, mimicking a line from Casablanca. "Is it just a coincidence?"

"I do not believe in coincidences; you should know that," Anya smiled. "Please place him in the room adjacent to mine," she instructed the desk clerk, who nodded in acknowledgment.

The feelings running through Jacob's head were confusing as he struggled to sort out all the questions he had for Anya. One part of his psyche was pleased that she was there, not acting like an adversary but as an old friend, interested in Jacob and wanting more conversation. The other side of his emotional book told him to turn and walk away, but he knew that was not in the cards.

"I was about to order dinner and eat in my room. I hate to be alone, and I have so many questions to ask you. Would you like a meal sent up as well? After you have checked into your room and gotten comfortable, of course," she said, never taking her gaze from Jacob's eyes.

"It might be better to meet in public on the roof dining area. You understand, I'm sure," he said with a hint of suspicion in his voice.

"Of course, Jacob, I have to earn your trust, I understand. Let us say six o'clock?"

"Six o'clock it is. See you then," he said, turning to the desk clerk, leaving Anya standing and looking at the back of his head. Her two hands reached out, touching his shoulders with a slight squeeze. He could feel her body against his back, her head resting on him.

"I am so glad to see you again, Jacob," Anya whispered and turned to leave.

Jacob checked into his room, took a quick shower, and laid out the casual white, short-sleeved shirt and tan pants he planned to wear at dinner. The door on the wall of his room, behind the entry door, was shut. A two-way lock prevented either side from entering the other room unless both guests unlocked their side. Jacob left his side locked and was going to try the doorknob; however, this made him concerned that if Anya heard the doorknob being turned, she might interpret this as interest by Jacob in entering her room, and he wanted that thought avoided for a while longer.

As a security measure, Jacob tore off a small piece of bathroom tissue paper, the size of his thumbnail, and folded it into quarters. Gently placing the paper near the bottom of the door in the gap between the frame and the door, Jacob gently pushed the piece of tissue into the crack. If anyone opened the door after he left, the paper would fall loose onto the floor, indicating the door had been opened. A piece of tissue the size of half a stamp would not be noticed lying innocently on the floor. He prepared a second piece identical to the first. As he left his room, Jacob made sure no one else was present and then quickly placed the second paper in the door frame as he had done moments before. This would tell him if his main room door had been opened while he was at dinner. Stone had taught him small but useful tips that were never in his academy training.

Jacob stepped out onto the terrace of the fourth-floor Lux Lucis restaurant, scanning the area in search of Anya's presence. Not spotting her, the host guided Jacob to a small table at the restaurant's corner. From this vantage point, a breathtaking panorama unfolded before him—on one side, the majestic Apuan Alps, and on the other, the azure expanse of the Tyrrhenian Sea. A gentle ocean breeze wafted through, carrying a faint hint of Anya's familiar perfume. As Jacob turned, he beheld Anya walking towards him, seemingly moving in a graceful, slow motion. Adorned in an enchanting full-length dress, she exuded an ethereal charm that perfectly complemented the gentle sway of the fabric in the breeze. The dress, crafted from lightweight and flowing chiffon, featured a subtle V-neckline that delicately accentuated her collarbones. Delicate spaghetti straps added an element of fragility to the overall design. The bodice embraced her figure elegantly, tracing her silhouette before cascading into a softly flared skirt that gracefully trailed along the floor. A profound sense of yearning and desire surged through Jacob as if time itself had momentarily suspended. The combination of Anya's captivating allure and the dress's otherworldly quality forged an atmosphere akin to a magical fairy tale, evoking memories of when he had embarked on a perilous journey for love.

"You look stunning, as usual," he said flirtatiously.

"Thank you, Jacob. You also look very handsome tonight," she smiled at him.

This restaurant was known for its Michelin Star rating, and tonight, Jacob and Anya were about to put it to the test. After a cocktail and some light conversation, the waiter came to take their orders. Anya chose the Mediterranean grilled black fish with a glass of 2019 Toscana Bianco, Sauvignon Blanc. Jacob chose the eggs with mantis shrimp, wild herbs, sansho pepper, black truffle, and a glass of 2011 Riesling Mosel Uhlen Roth Lay to accompany his dinner. As the meal was served, the restaurant Sommelier approached the table and expressed his appreciation for their wine pairing, which was an excellent choice. After leaving the table, Jacob looked at Anya.

"I wonder if they realize I opened the wine menu, closed my eyes, and put my finger on the page. It could have been chocolate milk I selected; who knew?" The two exchanged a moment of humor.

"I like this," Anya said. "Just like when we were together. All those nasty, cruel things I said to you, I did not mean any of them. I was acting out a script," she said, her eyes having that familiar puppy-like look he remembered from the past. And now he took the role of a thespian.

"Why couldn't you have just told your father you refused to do it," referring to her attempted murder of Jacob by having him thrown off their ship.

"You don't know my father as I do. I once saw him use a cheese slicer to remove the skin of a man from whom he wanted information. I was only thirteen years old, and he did not know I saw this, but it changed my opinion of him. Watching the poor man die so slowly and in such agony. I am terrified of him, as is my mother." Anya's face was serious, and her hand was resting on her lap, shaking. Jacob reached over the table, touching Anya's other hand.

"I understand now. I'm so sorry you have had to live with that fear," he said, his eyes watering. Anya gave a slight smile to indicate her appreciation of his sincerity.

"But that still doesn't answer the question, why are you here?" Jacob asked.

"I wanted to have time to talk alone. No Federal partners, no fathers wanting to listen in, just you and me."

"And you just thought I might be at this hotel in this town, in this country, during this week," he said, wanting a convincing answer from her.

"As you have sources, so do I. And it looks like they were right," she said, lifting her glass as if to toast.

Jacob accepted her explanation. She had a father who could pay any amount for information, and it was apparent that Anya used those sources for her good. But then Jason got serious.

"Anya, whose idea was it to kill Lisa," referring to his ex-girlfriend who had been shot in front of the Ferry building in San Francisco. Jacob had been told that Anya hired the men to keep Lisa from getting married to Jacob, thereby preventing Anya from inheriting the Anastasia Dream once Jacob was dead.

"As my father said in his papers to the court, it was his plan," she said, looking straight into Jacob's eyes.

And there it was, blaming Daddy for all the bad things that happened. This was too easy an explanation. But Daddy did take care of the loose ends, having any witness who worked for Anya killed in prison. Peter could confess to anything; if there was no corroborating evidence to the contrary, he was a free man. With so many enemies, Peter had no intention of returning to the United States. Now, there were bigger concerns, with contacts in the Kremlin doubting his loyalty.

As dinner and dessert finished, Anya and Jacob sat around the fire pit to enjoy a cocktail before returning to their room. While they walked through the lobby, Anya reached over and took Jacob's hand, squeezing it. He was all right with her sign of affection; she was comfortable holding the hand of a Federal Agent.

They made their way to their rooms, and at the door, they paused for a moment. Anya put her arm around him with her face inches from his. He had always been mesmerized by this woman's bright green eyes. Her breathing was increasing as she pushed her hips closer to his.

"Would you like to come in and talk about old times?" she said in a whisper.

It was hard to resist her advancement, and he knew that they would spend hours in bed together being the sexual dynamos they were back on the ship, but he had to restrain himself, at least for tonight.

"I don't think we are ready yet, I need some time," he said reluctantly.

Anya rested her head on his chest and let out a large sigh.

"I understand. You go take a cold shower, and I will take a warm bath, and we can imagine what the night would have been like," She pulled away and smiled, giving Jacob a slow, soft kiss, which he accepted without hesitation.

Anya entered her room, and Jacob followed suit, intentionally observing as she closed the door. Afterward, he checked the paper tracer that he had discreetly placed in the door earlier—it remained undisturbed, as did the one lodged in the adjoining door connecting his room to Anya's. With an early morning ahead, Jacob had to meet his contact from IFCACC at a local office they had recently established just outside Forte del Marmi. Given that Russian oligarchs frequently visited this town, arriving in yachts and helicopters, many of which were subsequently seized under the sanctions program, it served as an ideal location for their operations.

The sun rose an hour after Jacob had showered, and he found himself standing at the hotel entrance, awaiting the car he had requested. As the Mercedes pulled up, the driver introduced himself by presenting a business card. Jacob handed him a small piece of paper containing an address and proceeded to open the back door of the luxurious vehicle. During the ten-minute drive, Jacob had the opportunity to catch glimpses of the local villages. He was particularly struck by the meticulously maintained lawns and the stunning Italian mansions concealed behind verdant hedges. Both sides of the street were adorned with cement paver sidewalks, but as he approached the city limit, the sidewalks abruptly transitioned to dirt. Finally, the car stopped in front of an unassuming building enclosed by a metal gate. Closed Circuit Television Cameras were strategically positioned to monitor the sole entrance point, and underneath one of the cameras, a small square box with a numeric keypad was mounted.

Jacob approached the gate and examined the unfamiliar keypad, trying to figure out how to proceed. As he glanced up at the camera above, a buzzing sound emanated from the gate, indicating that someone had noticed his presence and unlocked it for him. Jacob pushed on the gate, which swung open, revealing a pathway adorned with vibrant Italian tiles. At the end of the path stood a large, weathered wooden door with an arched top. The door swung open before Jacob could even knock, revealing a young woman with long black hair and bangs elegantly framing her forehead. She greeted Jacob with a warm smile.

"Agent Westerly?" she asked.

"Yes, Jacob Westerly, I am here to see," Jacob fumbled with his phone, looking at the notes app. "Alessandro Bianchi," I hope I pronounced that correctly, Jacob inquired.

"Perfectly, please come and follow me," the young lady turned and proceeded towards the back of the building as Jacob followed, trying his best not to allow his eyes to wander. They approached a wooden door, and the young woman knocked on it with two quick raps.

"Entrare," a male voice called out from behind the door.

The woman opened the door and stood to the side as Jacob entered. Out of the corner of his eye, he could see the woman evaluating him, and he passed within inches of her. His nose picked up the scent of her Dior perfume, which seemed to linger with him as he entered the room. The man behind the desk stood and walked around with his hand outstretched.

"Alessandro Bianchi, Agente di Polizia di Interpol. And you must be Agent Jacob Westerly, welcome to Italy," he greeted Jacob.

Alessandro Bianchi, a 38-year-old native of Florence, Italy, was a seasoned police officer with extensive experience in law enforcement. Growing up in a family of dedicated public servants, Alessandro was instilled with a strong sense of justice and a desire to make a difference in the world. His exceptional investigative skills, combined with his multilingual abilities, led him to a distinguished career with Interpol. He also had a weakness for beautiful assistants and fine cocktails.

"I was so sorry to hear that Agent Stone would not be accompanying you; he sounds like an interesting person, I would have enjoyed making his acquaintance," Alessandro said, directing Jacob to a seat. "I understand you might be able to assist us in the mystery of our document."

"Yes, I hope so. Where did you get this document?" already knowing where it was found, but testing his host's memory.

"A Russian oligarch, Maxim Volkov. He has a home in Forte del Marmi and owns a Caviar company in Moscow. When the sanctions were imposed, we received information from an unknown informant that Volkov had several rare documents and paintings. We searched his home and discovered a rare painting, Madonna and Child, painted around 1290–1300 by Duccio di Buoninsegna, who died in 1318. The painting was stolen from your Metropolitan Museum of Art several years ago. He also had several stolen Roman coins and vases, but the most interesting document found was a private land grant from Mussolini to Hitler before the start of World War II. This document was unknown to the world, and he was preparing to auction the document off at Christie's when our informant was shown the paper."

Alessandro retrieved two sets of white cotton gloves from his drawer and handed a pair to Jacob. They both donned the gloves, and Alessandro proceeded to unlock a metal box. From within the box, he retrieved a folder adorned with the Interpol emblem—a world surrounded by leaves with a sword positioned vertically behind the globe. Alessandro gingerly opened the folder, taking out a meticulously preserved document. The paper had a vintage appearance, with a brownish hue, and featured typewritten text in both Italian and German. Adjacent to the signature, a handwritten date appeared to be from 1934.

The item was gently handed to Jacob, who placed it on the table in front of him and removed his cell phone. Opening an app that magnified and recorded images in front of the phone, Jacob took a photo. The app showed a rotating hourglass as it worked; it stopped as Jacob read the text.

"Just as I suspected, a forgery," Jacob said, turning off his app, returning his phone, and placing it in his pocket.

"A forgery? How can you be so sure?" Alessandro asked, his voice hinting at doubt.

"Very simple, see the font style? This font is called American Typewriter; it is a serif typeface classified as a slab serif. A slab serif font is a serif font where the serifs, the slight projections that finish off the strokes of letters, are squared off, giving the font a blocky, sturdy appearance as opposed to the more refined look of a traditional serif. It was created in 1974 by two men, Joel Kaden and Tony Stan for the International Typeface Corporation. This typeface was used primarily on American-built typewriters." Looking around the room, Jacob noticed a small typewriter displayed on a shelf behind the desk; the brand name Olivetti was printed on the front of the machine. He gently removed the antique typewriter, placing it on the desk.

"May I have a blank piece of paper?" Jacob asked the young lady who opened a desk drawer, handing a sheet of paper to the agent.

Jacob placed the paper in the feed roller of the typewriter, gently rolling the paper using the platen knob, into the machine, stopping when it was aligned behind the type guide.

Jacob positioned the document beside the typewriter and proceeded to press the manual keys, meticulously typing out the first sentence as it appeared on the document. After a brief pause, he examined the text he had just typed. Retrieving his cell phone, he activated an app and held the phone up, aligning it with the line of text he had entered. Within moments, the results appeared on the phone's screen, prompting Jacob to nod in approval subtly.

"This typeface is from a 1961 Olivetti Studio 44 typewriter," tapping his hand on the machine in front of him. The application I used is very accurate; however, there is one additional piece of evidence you should be aware of:" Jacob removed the paper from the typewriter, laying it next to the document in question. "Run your fingers over the first line of the Mussolini document, removing it from the protective plastic insert.

Alessandro removed his white glove and gently ran his finger over the document. Jacob moved the documents he had just typed in front of Alessandro.

"Do the same to this one," Jacob instructed Alessandro

The man once again slid his finger over the sentence that was typed. With a bewildered look on his face, he slowly raised his head, looking at Jacob in confusion.

"The Mussolini document is smooth to the touch, yet your typewritten document is indented and rough. It is a forgery," Alessandro announced, dropping his head in disgust. "I am sorry, Agent Westerly, for wasting your valuable time."

A copy of the same document lay on the table near Jacob. Alessandro's assistant originally handed this to Jacob, under the misguided assumption that the original would not be used and a copy would suffice. Jacob glanced at the copy, thinking that it could be helpful if he needed to take the original. He placed his notepad over the copy, as a magician would do during a performance using sleight of hand. "Misdirect the mark's field of view," he thought to himself.

Jacob remained silent, reaching into his pocket to retrieve a small metal box with a hinged top. With the insertion of the USB cable from the device into his cell phone, the

Nanopore MinION Mk1C sprang to life. The activation of the MinKNOW software displayed a "READY" message on the cell phone screen. Jacob then carefully donned a pair of latex gloves, extracting a one-inch square cotton wipe from its container using his right hand. Alessandro and his assistant observed with curiosity as Jacob executed each step with precision. Holding the document in his left hand, Jacob methodically swabbed the edges using his right hand. Once finished, he opened the small lid of the MinION, placing the swab on a designated indentation in the plastic before closing the lid. Removing his gloves, Jacob pressed the "START" button on the cell phone application. Moments later, as he read the readout on his cell phone, he couldn't believe what he saw. The results were both shocking and, at the same time, expected.

On the car ride back to the hotel, Jacob removed the protected document from his suit jacket pocket. In a quick slide of hand, he had removed the original document replacing it with the copy that was originally handed to him. He figured it would be hours before the Italian official discovered the switch. He needed the original as evidence.

CHAPTER 13 (Assassin)

As the man ascended the stairs to the rooftop, his heart pounded with anticipation. Every step was a silent countdown to the moment of truth. Years of relentless training had honed his body to perfection, ensuring that fatigue was a foreign concept to him now.

Upon reaching the rooftop, he moved with the grace of a predator stalking its prey. Every motion was calculated, every breath controlled. He crouched low as he approached the roofs edge, his senses on high alert for any sign of detection.

The city sprawled out below him, a maze of streets and buildings that would soon become his hunting ground. With a sense of purpose, he unzipped the bag slung over his shoulder, revealing the deadly contents within.

The VSS Vintorez sniper rifle emerged from its concealment, its sleek design a testament to its lethal capabilities. With steady hands, he positioned the rifle on the edge of the building, ensuring it had a stable base from which to strike. A small sandbag was placed beneath the barrel, a makeshift rest to steady his aim when the moment came.

As he prepared his weapon, the sniper's mind raced with calculations and considerations. He noted the wind direction and the heat of the day, factors that could mean the difference between success and failure. With practiced ease, he adjusted the settings on his scope, fine-tuning his aim for maximum precision.

Behind the tinted lenses of his sunglasses, his eyes narrowed with focus. This was his domain, his realm of expertise. Each kill was a testament to his skill, a testament to the years of dedication and sacrifice he had poured into his craft.

At another time, he might have favored his Dragunov Sniper rifle, but circumstances dictated otherwise. His contact in Italy had failed to procure the weapon in time, leaving him with no choice but to rely on the VSS for this particular job.

But he was not deterred. Although the weapon had changed, his resolve remained unwavering. With a steady hand and a steely gaze, he waited for his target to appear, knowing that when the moment came, he would be ready. For he was not just a sniper—he was a master of his trade, a ghost in the shadows, a force to be reckoned with. And tonight, someone would pay the ultimate price for crossing his path.

He meticulously inserted the earbuds into his ears, ensuring the perfect fit before initiating the music app on his cellphone. With a deliberate tap, the haunting melodies of Prokofiev's Violin Sonata No. 1, Op. 80, filled his consciousness, wrapping him in a cocoon of tranquility. As the soothing strains enveloped him, he adjusted the scope of the rifle with practiced precision, his movements fluid yet methodical.

The music acted as a portal, transporting him to a distant realm where memories lay dormant yet vivid. In the depths of his mind, he wandered through sun-kissed shores where laughter echoed like distant thunder. Recollections of cherished moments flooded his senses, memories of tender evenings spent with his beloved wife and daughter, their silhouettes dancing against the backdrop of a setting sun. Together, they reveled in the simple joys of life, relishing in the warmth of each other's company as they savored the fruits of the sea, their feast a symphony of flavors and aromas.

But beneath the surface of nostalgia lurked a shadow, a specter of regret that haunted his every thought. Their untimely demise, a cruel twist of fate orchestrated by the hands of negligence, weighed heavily on his conscience. He couldn't shake the nagging guilt that gnawed at his soul, a relentless reminder of his perceived failure as a husband and father. If only he had been more attentive, more vigilant in safeguarding their happiness, perhaps tragedy could have been averted.

Yet amidst the turmoil of remorse, duty called out to him like a siren's song, pulling him back from the abyss of introspection. This assignment, shrouded in secrecy and sanctioned by unseen forces, demanded his unwavering allegiance. Bound by an oath he dared not defy, he treaded the precarious path laid out by his enigmatic superiors, his allegiance tethered to the promise of redemption.

For him, sanctuary could not exist until the mission was complete, and solace could not exist until the scales of justice were balanced. With each heartbeat, he teetered on the edge of uncertainty, grappling with the weight of his dual existence. Failure was not an option; the consequences were too dire to contemplate. To falter would mean exile, a fate far worse than death.

And so, with resolve hardened like steel, he steadied his grip on the rifle, his senses attuned to the rhythmic pulse of the music that now served as both his shield and his sword. In the crucible of fate, he stood as a solitary sentinel, his fate intertwined with the whims of fate, his destiny a tapestry woven with threads of secrecy and sacrifice.

His target was walking around in the room, never stopping long enough to make the shot count. A man was also in the room, sometimes stepping in front of the window, blocking the shot. The shooter did not want to risk trying a shot at the man, with hopes it would penetrate his body and kill the woman. The man appeared concerned and walked over, picking up the telephone and calling a number. The woman stepped in direct line of sight. The first round fired caused the window to explode in a fury of glass. He waited as the woman was no longer in sight. His mind told him that the shot was successful, but moments later the man's shoulder appeared in the frame of the broken window. The man at the window quickly lifted his hand, he was holding a gun. The assassin could only see the muzzle flashes and, moments later, the sound of the shots, one, two, three rounds fired indiscriminately; what was the man at the window hoping to accomplish? Not seeing the woman again, the assassin prepared to quickly leave, his job was finished, and so was he. A single round to the back of the head and the assassin slumped to the ground, he was dead. The person who shot him took no time in recovering the rifle and the ejected cartridge that the assassin discarded by racking the bolt action of the rifle, preparing for a second shot if needed. The assassin lay bleeding out on the ground. The handgun used to shoot the assassin was strategically placed next to him.

Jacob unlocked his door and threw down his jacket. Disgusted that he had missed lunch for a useless meeting he opened his refrigerator, removing and popping the top off a cold Peroni brand beer. He took three large gulps when a knock at his door came. He had just unlocked the door adjoining his and Anya's room in anticipation that she would make an appearance. Opening the door, he found Anya standing in front of him, wearing her swimsuit and towel wrapped around her waist. Her hair was wet and brushed back, indicating she had been in the pool.

"I was hoping you would come over and have a beer with me, but it looks like you've already started," she said, frowning.

"I can use a second; let me toss this one." As he turned to throw it in the trash, his eye noticed something. The piece of paper he had placed in the frame of the door adjoining the two rooms was on the floor. Someone had entered his room while he was away. He walked to the closet, where a wall safe was attached. Punching in four numbers and the hashtag, the door bolts securing the safe door came to life. He opened the door.

"Son of a bitch, someone's been in my room," he said angrily. Walking to the phone he paused, deciding not to touch the phone in case it needed to be processed for fingerprints.

"What is wrong, Jacob?" Anya asked from the still-opened door.

"My work gun is missing. Someone got into my safe and took it. I need to use your phone," as he turned to walk next door to Anya's room.

"Of course," Anya said with concern.

Anya placed the key card on her room door lock and opened the door, walking in with Jacob following.

"Who do you think could have done this? Did you not set your code before shutting it?" She knew what she was talking about, as Jacob drifted back, remembering an event on his ship when Anya was attempting to break into their room safe as the combination was unknown and the ship's engineer could not force it open. As they stood in the main room discussing the situation, Jacob moved to the phone, preparing to call the front desk and demand answers. Anya turned just as the window exploded behind her. Glass filled the room, and the mirror on the wall shattered on the couch. Anya dropped to the floor as Jacob yelled her name. No reply.

There was no blood around Anya as she started to stand.

"NO, stay down," as Anya remained on the floor with her hands over, her head, covered in broken glass.

The sea air filled the room, moving the curtains and partially blocking the window view. Jacob realized that he was still armed with his backup gun in his ankle holster. He unholstered the gun, holding it down and facing the floor as he took three deep breaths and calculated his next move. He peered around the corner of the curtain and immediately saw the sun's reflection off a small piece of glass on the rooftop across the field. The sunlight was flickering as if the glass was moving ever so slightly. He paused and then rotated around the broken window frame, shooting off three quick bursts from his Glock G43 9mm automatic handgun. He returned to the cover of the wall, signaling Anya to remain down on the floor. After 5 minutes of no more gunshots and the sounds of sirens in the distance, Jacob quickly moved to Anya, taking her hand as they ran to the hallway. They stopped and stood there in each other's arms, breathing rapidly.

"Are you ok?" He asked while looking over her head and body.

"Yes, my hero. You saved my life," she said, wrapping her arms around his neck and hugging him.

Jacob could smell Anya's perspiration, which told him that she was not prepared for what had just occurred in the room moments before. He, too, was shaken, but he did not want to show it.

"We need to get out of here. My uncle has a villa not far from here. We will be safe there until we can decide what to do," Anya said with desperation in her voice.

"I think we should stay here and wait for the police," Jacob said

"Are you kidding me, Jacob? An assassin just tried to kill me or maybe missed you after you just returned from visiting someone important to your work, why?" She asked insistently.

Jacob stood there and thought for a moment. "Ok let's go. Get your stuff and I'll grab my paperwork," as he turned to enter his room. Anya grabbed a sundress, shoes, her bag, and sunglasses. They walked down the emergency stairs to avoid anyone and onto the street. A few moments later, Anya saw a cab approaching and raised her hand to signal the car. It pulled over, and the two of them drove off. Approaching from the opposite direction, two Italian police cars passed at a high rate of speed with their lights and sirens blaring. The two passengers looked towards the floorboard, hiding their faces.

CHAPTER 14 (Setup)

The phone call to Stone came late at night while he was sleeping. The cell phone on the nightstand buzzed, eventually stirring Stone awake. Stone reached over in the darkness, fumbling for his glasses, eventually placing them on and looking at the cell phone display. BENNETT displayed on the screen that the time was 1:00 a.m. in Germany, so Stone made a quick calculation that it must be 7:00 p.m. in Washington, D.C. Odd, he thought; why would the Assistant Director of FinCEN be calling after hours? Stone pushed the answer button.

"Director Bennett, Stone here. It's awfully late to be calling me for a good night wish." Stone felt the early morning sarcasm was warranted.

"Wake your ass up and let me know when you are ready for some unpleasant info," Bennett warned Stone.

"Go ahead," Stone rubbed his eyes.

"Our boy, or should I say your boy, is a traitor," Bennett said with anger.

Stone rubbed his eyes and sat up on the edge of his bed. "What do you mean he's a traitor?" Trying to wake up and listen to what Bennett thought he knew.

"Italian Interpol just contacted me to say there is a warrant for Westerly's arrest. Apparently, he killed some guy on a rooftop of a building, and he's running with that Russian bitch of a wife."

"What? Who Anya? That's his ex-wife. He got a voicemail message from an AG saying she had been released over a technicality and then showed up at the hospital in Hamburg as we were interviewing her father," Stone explained, sliding on his glasses.

"Well, he still has a spark for her. I've sent you a couple of photos taken by the Italians when they discovered she was checked into the same hotel as Westerly. I never thought I should have listened to you about putting him in the FinCEN Unit. He likes that good life after the boat incident and now he decided to get back in with the woman who can make him more money, SHIT!" Bennett said as if just about to lose his temper.

"Who was this guy on the roof? How do we know Jacob had anything to do with it?" This piece of information was what Stone was curious about.

"The Italians found his service gun on the other side of the roof, several rounds had been shot, and Westerly's fingerprints were all over it. They figure he got into a struggle with someone else on the roof and lost his gun before escaping. He never even checked out of the hotel; he and the girl are gone," Bennet explained.

Stone did find this story odd, as Jacob had not checked in after leaving for the Italian police agency. Stone was not concerned with Bennett's information and the story the Italians were providing.

"Jacob was supposed to meet with Alessandro Bianchi, of the Italian Interpol Office…" he was cut short as Bennett interrupted him.

"Yeah, that's another thing, Westerly made his appointment but then stole a rare document worth a million. This guy just can't keep himself away from the valuable stuff, and now he's hooked up with that Russian tart. What a shit show you created by trusting him. We have several teams out looking for the two of them," Bennett said forcefully.

"I'll be on the next plane to Florence," Stone assured Bennett.

"NO! I have a C5 waiting for you at Ramstein. Get packed and get back here, you're no good to me in Germany," the phone hung up with a slam.

Stone looked at the text messages Bennett had sent. Several photos showed Jacob and Anya having dinner, her hugging him behind at the hotel desk, and kissing in a hotel hallway. Stone sat there looking at the photos and turned off the screen. Removing his satellite phone from the drawer, Stone walked over to the sliding glass door to the balcony. He opened it and activated the phone. He dialed the number to Jacob's satellite phone he provided before Jacob left for Italy. The phone rang. No answer; however, Stone was not concerned. His attempted call would tell Jacob what he needed to know.

◆　◆　◆

"Pull over here," Anya instructed the driver.

The cab driver pulled over on a single-lane country road, awaiting further instructions. Anya handed the driver cash and checked the app on her phone. The rolling hills were covered in vineyards, with green leaves and tight bunches of grapes waiting for the farmhands to arrive and begin the picking, which would eventually be processed into various varietals of red and white wines. The sun was beginning to set as Jacob and Anya grabbed their small bags from the car. They were alone; nothing but fields surrounded them with smooth, finely crushed rock beneath their feet. Jacob looked at the cab as it drove off, leaving them standing there.

"Now what?" Jacob asked.

"We walk a bit, that way," Anya pointed towards the area the cab had driven off.

They made their way up a slight rise in the road, each carrying their small handbags. Jacob looked at Anya, who was determined and walking at a brisk pace. As they rounded a corner in the road, Anya paused. She opened her bag and reached inside, fumbling with something. Jacob quietly moved close and recognized what he was handling. A small, round noise suppressor, known to most as a silencer. With a few quick movements, she had attached the suppressor to the end of her handgun and placed it back in her purse.

"Really? A silencer for your gun, what exactly are you getting ready for?" Jacob asked with concern in his voice.

"Consider me your guardian angel. My job is to make sure we get to my uncle's villa," she said, turning and beginning to walk again.

They picked up their pace, walking quickly on the long, desolate road. As they cleared the top of the rise in the road, the sound of a car on the gravel approached from behind. Over the crest of the hill came a small, four-door blue car with a small light bar on the roof and a white stripe across the door, bearing the word "Polizia Municipale." The lone driver slowed as the car approached. Jacob stopped walking and turned his attention to the solo officer who had activated the blue light bar on top of the car. Anya continued to walk as the officer slowly got out of his car.

"Mi scusi signorina, si prega di tornare, *(Excuse me Miss please return),* the officer announced while keeping a watchful eye on Jacob.

Anya slowed yet kept walking as she slowly placed her right hand into the shoulder bag she was carrying. A pair of wired earbuds in her ears, the wire leading into her bag.

"Signorian fermata ora! *(Miss, stop now!)* The officer yelled.

Anya stopped, still looking forward. She slowly turned and stopped, shrugging her shoulders as if questioning the officer with body language.

The officer raised his left hand, signaling with his palm to return. Anya understood the order, and she slowly made her way back with a look of disapproval. Jacob remained stationary, watching Anya's unusual behavior.

"Grazie, da dove ventite voi due?" *(Thank you, where are you two coming from?)* he asked Jacob and Anya as he closed his door and placed his hat strategically on his head, taking time to position the white high-front hat with the greatest precision.

"I'm sorry, but I don't know Italian. Do you speak English?" Jacob asked, raising his hand slightly but being careful not to make any furtive gestures that might be interpreted wrong.

The officer turned his attention to Anya, who was standing a few feet to the right of Jacob. She also shrugged her shoulder, indicating that she did not understand what the officer was saying.

"Very well, I will speak in English," he said.

"Thank you. We are lost and trying to find the local village," Anya said, her eyes a puppy-like look and her head slightly tilted.

"Yes, mam, I can help you and your husband with that," the officer said, smiling at Anya.

"Oh no, he is not my husband, just a man I am traveling with," Anya said with a coy look, knowing the officer was showing a slight bit of interest, as she slowly walked towards him.

The officer, feeling a bit more at ease with the young woman, stepped out from behind his door and walked towards her.

"Do you have friends or relatives in the village?" He asked.

Anya moved within a few feet of him. Jacob could see the officer's nostrils on his nose expand, and he could only imagine that he was letting his olfactory senses enjoy Anya's perfume. Anya put her hand to her ear, removing the earbud and slipping her hand into her purse. Jacob assumed she was turning off the music on her cell phone, but he soon discovered his error.

Anya reached out gently, placing her hand on the officer's chest, which momentarily stunned him, as a slight smile spread across his mouth. As his glance dropped to her hand on his chest, Anya's right hand quickly came out of her purse, now holding a small automatic handgun with a silencer attached. She pushed hard, which caused the officer to fall off balance, his body striking the corner of the car. His hand reached for the weapon on his belt; however, the timing was not to his advantage. Anya raised the gun and, before Jacob could react, placed two quick shots in the officer's chest. He fell to the road, not saying a word.

"Anya!" Jacob yelled as he crouched.

But Anya was calm and knew exactly what she planned to do. She took two steps towards the fallen officer, raised her weapon, and gave one last shot to the forehead of the unconscious man lying next to his car, the engine still running and the light bar on the roof rotating.

"What the fuck, Anya. Why did you shoot him?" Jacob yelled.

"I didn't like how he was looking at me. It was like he was trying to lure me away from you," she said comically.

Jacob, not knowing what or how she could do this, tried to figure out what to do next. Anya reached down and took the portable handheld police radio from the dead man's belt.

"This will come in handy. Let's go," she said as she stood, placing her gun and the radio in her purse. And continued walking with Jacob standing and staring at the dead officer on the side of the road.

"Anya, we just can't leave. You shot this guy!" Jacob yelled to her as he paced around, trying to decide what to do.

"Jacob, my love, if you stay, you will go to jail. They will say you are responsible, that is, if the next police officer to arrive is not being paid to find you and complete the job from the hotel. Hurry up, our ride is coming soon," Anya continued to walk, and Jacob, thinking about the logic of her statement, decided that maybe she was right. He turned and ran until he caught up with her.

They walked another half mile, turning east on the next county street they came to. Jacob was sweating, and his breathing was fast; he felt that he might pass out at any moment. He stopped and bent over, trying to catch his breath.

"Hold on, hold on one moment. I need to catch my breath," he begged her.

"I thought you secret agents were all in tip-top shape, Agent Westerly?" a hint of sarcasm in her voice.

"Special Agent. It's I'm a Special Agent," Jacob said, correcting her.

"If you say so, Special Agent guy. Not to worry, our ride is here," turning her back to Jacob as a car approached and slowed.

With this last shooting and the one before, he was concerned that they had not stayed at the hotel to answer questions and that this would appear as if they were criminals trying to evade the authorities. Should I call Stone, he wondered? No, that would not be a wise thing to do. His hand felt the outside of his right pocket to make sure that the Sat phone was still with him. It was.

The sound of an approaching car behind them made Anya stop her pace and concentrate on the vehicle. A black Mercedes E350 was slowing down as if to come to a stop. A lone driver wearing sunglasses flashed the lights twice. Anya looked at her phone screen and turned to Jacob.

"Our Uber has arrived," she said with a smile. The large emblem, in the shape of a U, appeared on the driver's side of the window. Anya looked at the driver's face and then compared it to the image on her Uber app. She opened the rear door and looked at Jacob, who was still standing motionless on the side of the road, watching the event unfold.

"Well, are you going to get in or walk to the villa?" Anya said sarcastically.

Jacob opened the opposite rear door, throwing in his bag and joining Anya. As the car drove off, Anya leaned forward and handed the driver several fifty-dollar bills in U.S. cash.

"You just picked up two black men whose car had broken down and dropped them off in the village, understand?" she said while looking at the man's eyes in the mirror. The driver reached back, took the bills, and nodded his head after a quick examination of the money.

"Sì signorina, ho capito," *(Yes, miss, I get it)* he replied.

Anya leaned back into the seat, taking Jacob's hand as he stared at her, amazed at what he had just witnessed. This was a side of Anya he had never seen. So confident and actually very hot, he thought to himself. They drove for forty minutes, making several turns until they reached a small entrance road with a black rod iron gate. Anya reached into her bag, removed a remote-control fob, and pressed the button. The gate slowly rose, allowing the driver to continue up through the hills. As they rounded the corner, Jacob could see the three-story Italian villa nestled amidst vast acres of lush wine vineyards, creating a picturesque setting that exuded charm and tranquility. Approaching the home, Jacob's attention was immediately drawn to the grand fountain situated at the center of the driveway. The villa's large front doors were a testament to the natural beauty and history that pervaded the estate. Crafted meticulously from old trees, they possess a distinct character and charm, showcasing the work of skilled artisans who sought to preserve the essence of the surrounding environment. These doors offered a warm invitation to enter, hinting at the treasures that awaited within.

The moment they got out of the Mercedes, Jacob thought he saw Anya place something small in the pouch behind the driver's seat, where magazines are normally kept. It appeared to be a small box with an LED light glowing. His mind immediately rationalized that Anya was tracking the driver, probably concerned that he might go to the authorities and report the two fugitives he had just transported. She is a smart lady, he thought to himself.

Jacob and Anya approached the front doors. Anya walked into the foyer and looked around the corner of the arch. A small keypad with a red light was located just below a dome pod housing a miniature camera. Anya pressed several keys that chirped as she depressed them, eventually signaling with five chirps that the correct code had been entered; a green light activated where there had once been a red one. As they stepped up to the entrance area, preparing to enter the front doors, a loud explosion could be heard in the distance. They turned to see a plume of black smoke rising into the sky. Jacob instantly knew what it was.

"I thought his car was running a bit rough," Anya said without emotion.

Turning and opening the large wooden door. Jacob stood there, looking at the smoke, as he slowly turned and watched as Anya walked into the villa's entryway. Now, more than ever, he had to keep a close eye on this woman, as it was apparent what she was capable of.

Jacob followed Anya into the entryway of the Italian-style villa. Concerned that others may be present, Jacob scanned to his sides and up the curling staircase that led to other rooms on the second floor. Framed photographs hung on the walls, depicting groups of both men and women posing for the camera. One he recognized was Mikhail Gorbachev, President of the Soviet Union from 1989 to 1991. Jacob did not recognize the man shaking hands with Gorbachev. However, the location in which they took the photo had the same background as the vineyards Jacob had seen while driving into the villa.

"I am beaten. Let's have some wine," Anya said as she examined bottles from the floor-to-roof wine closet that blended into the cabinetry of the kitchen.

Jacob felt uneasy about any location where Anya was comfortable. He remembered her saying the villa belonged to her uncle and that concerned Jacob. Jacob casually reached down as he sat on the large, overstuffed couch, feeling his ankle holster to confirm that his Glock G43 was present and secure, ready if needed.

"Don't worry, my love. You won't need that here," Anya said as she handed Jacob a glass of red wine and sat next to him. She had retrieved a first aid kit and was attending to glass cuts on her knees and feet that she had suffered when she had fallen to the ground at the hotel.

"Anya, you're bleeding," Jacob said with concern, dropping to his knees and examining Anya's wounds.

Anya reached up, stroking the hair on the side of Jacob's head. For a moment, she did not feel the pain of Jacob removing shards of glass with a pair of tweezers and dabbing up the blood. She felt different, like the time they bumped into each other at the Farmers Market in San Francisco. Although she knew back then she had an assignment, she still could not ignore the feelings she had when the two of them were close and personal.

Jacob bandaged as many wounds as he could of glass. He gently cleaned her leg with a damp paper towel, not touching the cuts. He looked up at Anya, and for a moment, they paused, lost in each other's gaze. Jacob pulled his attention away, sitting back on the couch.

"There, that should at least keep you from getting an infection. I'm sorry about all the bandages, but I needed to cover the wounds."

Jacob slowly took a sip of wine and paused for a moment, feeling the cool mouth feel of the liquid as he swallowed. He was impressed and raised his eyebrows to show his approval, looking at the glass in his hand.

"Very nice. Your uncle has excellent taste in wines. Was this from his vineyards outside?"

"No, no. My uncle purchased that bottle at an auction. It is from a vineyard in your Napa region, Stag's Leap Cellars. I believe he paid $12,300 for it, a wonderful Cabernet Sauvignon. He told me it beat the top Bordeaux in the 1976 Judgement of Paris tasting. Wonderful, don't you agree?" Anya slowly took a sip. Jacob nearly choked on the wine upon hearing the price.

"That glass of wine is worth around twenty-four hundred dollars, enjoy it!" Anya said with a smile, looking at Jacob.

"On the ride over, I thought I had better give Agent Stone a call and see if he had heard anything about our shooting incident," Jacob said as he lowered his glass to the table. Taking extra care with the expensive glass.

"I think that would be a bad idea, Jacob. They could track your phone to our location. And you being with me cannot look good," Anya said with concern.

Jacob stood and thought about the events that had just unfolded over the last eight hours. He looked out through the large glass windows, looking at his watch and noticing it was a couple of minutes before 4:00 p.m.

"Does your uncle have a television? I'd like to see if they have reported anything on the local stations." Jacob asked.

"Let's go to his home theater and I will see if I can remember how to operate the television," she said, standing and walking off with Jacob following.

Anya and Jacob walked into a spacious room located on the side of the villa. There were two dozen recliners, each with a small table between them. The theater architect had arranged the chairs in a cathedral-style seating, with each row elevated to provide the viewer behind the row with an unobstructed view of the large white screen on the wall in front of them. Jacob and Anya sat in the front row, with Anya holding the remote-control device.

Pressing a button on the remote control lit up the screen with an image of the villa, taken from a camera positioned on top of the roof, pointing towards the driveway. Her uncle had a security camera system that allowed a view around the villa in all directions, with zoom capabilities. Anya put down the remote and pressed several illuminated buttons on her armchair. The room lights dimmed, and the image on the screen changed to a televised signal. The logo of Rai News appeared on the screen. Moments later, the image of a young female news reporter sitting at a broadcast desk was visible. The woman was reading from a piece of paper in Italian and Jacob struggled to understand what she was saying until the image over her right shoulder appeared. Jacob sat forward, examining the image, his eyes wide open. It was his photograph taken at FLETC in Glynco, Georgia, during his training as a Federal Agent.

"Anya, do you understand Italian?" Jacob slowly said, still staring at the screen.

"Yes, Jacob, I do. And it is not good," Anya said while listening to the woman news reporter. "She is saying that Interpol wanted you for the murder of a man in Forte dei Marmi, that you executed on a rooftop. You stole a valuable document from the Interpol office that is worth millions of dollars, and you are armed and extremely dangerous." Anya looked at Jacob with concern.

"Are they saying anything about you?"

"No, apparently they have not connected us yet," she said, her attention fixed on the screen. "Your government has, as they say in America, 'kicked you under the cab,' Jacob. They don't give a shit about you or they would have corrected this story and proved your innocence." she said angrily.

"Kicked me under the bus," Jacob said

"God damn it, that is what I said. Stop correcting me, I am concerned about your safety. They tried to have you killed at the hotel, and now they blame you for some guy's death and accuse you of stealing a document. They are setting you up, Jacob, can't you understand?" Anya stood up, wincing at the pain in her legs. Limping to the window and looking outside, she shook her head with disgust.

"That's it. I'm going to put Stone on the spot. He needs to explain this." Jacob stood and removed his satellite phone from his pocket. He walked to the window, pointing the hinged antenna upward for a clear signal.

"Where did you get that phone?"

"This phone allows Stone and me to talk, without a trace or the NSA listening in. We didn't know who we could trust over here," pressing in a series of numbers.

"Well now, you really know who you cannot trust," Anya said sarcastically.

Moments later, Jacob pushed the speakerphone button so that Anya could hear their conversation.

"Westerly, where are you?" Stone asked in an authoritative voice.

"First, you tell me what the hell is going on, Stone. I just saw the news reports on TV. Why am I being blamed for this?"

"Are you with Anya?" Stone asked, and Jacob paused.

"Yes. What's it to you?"

"Listen, son. You need to go to the embassy and surrender yourself. Then we can talk more," Stone said, trying to be convincing.

"Why so they can lock me up in a black site? You tell me why I'm being hunted, and maybe I will see you again."

"They found your gun at the scene of a murder, Jacob. A security guard in the building was shot with it. How do you explain that? And the Italians told us that after you left your meeting, the document you had been examining had been switched. You kill a guy and steal documents? You need to come in and explain this. Before some special ops team finds you and makes the job quick and clean," Stone raised the volume so Jacob and Anya could hear.

"Fuck you, Stone. FUCK YOU!" Jacob ended the call. Jacob dropped the phone to the floor and put his head in his hands.

Anya walked over, sitting next to him on the couch, her hand rubbing his back.

"I thought these guys had my back. They always said, if you fuck up, don't worry, our people will sort it out and get you back on track. But they don't. They just keep lying to satisfy their agenda. I had a future, Anya. I could have worked at Treasury and retired with a great pension. Now I have nothing, and I'm probably going to spend my life at the same facility you did. Why are they determined to set me up? What did I do to deserve this?" Jacob said with his eyes tearing up.

"Don't worry, Jacob, the food at ADX is good, and I can set you up with Robert Hanssen, the American spy I used to play chess with," trying to make light of the situation.

"I need to get away from these people, quit being a Fed, and blend into the crowd."

"I can help you with that. My family is very well connected," Anya said as Jacob turned to look at her.

Anya slowly moved her face closer to Jacob's, giving him a gentle kiss on the lips. Jacob's eyes closed, his mind wandering back to this moment in San Francisco years ago when Anya surprised him with their first kiss. It still felt the same. She stood up and took his hand. They walked into a back bedroom and stood as Anya slowly undressed Jacob. Jacob was gentle, trying not to rub any of her wounds, but he found it hard as they made love for hours, falling asleep and returning to each other's arms, starting over again and again.

CHAPTER 15 (I'm with the band)

"I'm hungry," Anya said, rolling over and climbing on top of Jacob's naked body.

Jacob had just opened his eyes from a well-deserved nap. For a moment, he had a hard time recalling what he should do. The sun was setting, which added to his partial confusion. But having this beautiful green-eyed woman lying on top of him naked, gently kissing him, made everything unimportant. Her blond hair shrouded them both as they lay there, not speaking, just looking at each other.

Anya made a slight movement with her hips; a smile came to her face.

"Oh, Mr. Special Agent man, I see you are very much waking up," giving Jacob a soft kiss.

Jacob rolled onto his back and lay there looking at the ceiling. Anya could see his void and watched him.

"Why did you feel the need to kill that policeman?" he turned his attention to her.

Anya continued to examine her finger, which had the ring on it. Jacob could sense her delay in answering and wondered what kind of response she could have. The police officer posed no threat. Sure, maybe he was enjoying the flirting with this young, beautiful Russian girl, but this was no excuse to end his life. Jacob thought about the man's family and how they would react to the news of his death. What would his wife go through, and what if he had children? How would the mother break the news to them? Or worse yet, what if there was no mother in the picture and he was a single father struggling on a policeman's wage? These thoughts flashed through his mind at a record pace. Jacob could start to feel the temple on the right side of his head throb, and a small headache.

"We cannot take any chances. He might be one police officer, but he has a radio, which means he has many friends, also in uniform. In fact, his police family is worldwide when you think about it. If we were discovered, then both of us would be running for various reasons. And it's not like they just give up. I did what I had to do," as Anya threw the covers off her and rolled off the bed.

"You're comfortable with killing. It means nothing to you," he said with a bit of anger in his voice.

"I am not comfortable with it; I have just seen so much of it, I am…" She paused, searching for the correct meaning.

"Desensitized to it," Jacob replied.

Anya stopped and turned with a look on her face as if having never heard that word.

"De-what?"

"Desensitized. When you have done or seen something so many times, it does not affect you."

"Yeah, maybe, who knows, who cares. I'm hungry," she said sarcastically.

"Should we go into town and find a place to eat?" Jacob suggested as Anya walked into the bathroom.

"No, that would not be a good idea—two new faces, after a car explodes and a policeman is found shot. People will talk. Let's see what my uncle left behind," she said, opening the bathroom closet and searching through garments until she found a silk robe, which she tied around her waist.

"Regarding your uncle, I'm concerned that if the police know you are with me, as I assume my people will tell them, won't they look into your family and find your uncle's villa?"

"No, he purchased it with the help of a farmer who put the deed in his name. No one knows who my uncle is or his connection to this property," Anya said as she entered the kitchen and began her search through the cabinets.

Jacob opened the refrigerator that was hidden in the cabinetry with a similar cabinet door. Anya joined him, looking disappointed at what they had found.

"Some cheese, butter, bottled water, and a loaf of sourdough bread." She removed the bread and pulled some off, seeming surprised that it was still partially fresh. "Uncle Dmitri loved to grow tomatoes. Let me check out back." Anya opened the large glass door leading to a back deck behind the house that offered a view of the nearly setting sun over acres of grape vineyards.

Jacob removed an Alclad stainless steel pan from the overhead display of hanging pots and pans, placing it on the gas stove. Anya returned a few minutes later, carrying several Roma tomatoes and two garlic bulbs.

"I don't know what we can make with these, as there is no pasta," placing the bounty on the marble counter.

"You've never been a bachelor! Let me create for you the staple food of American college students, other than a keg of beer," Jacob started cutting the bread into slices along with the tomatoes. Anya was assigned the task of crushing the garlic cloves and then slicing thin strips of cheese. The butter and garlic were melted together in a small saucepan, and a brush was used to coat the bread with the garlicky butter.

"First, you gently arrange the cheese slices in a row. Not too many, not too few, taking care not to bruise them," he said jokingly, which took Anya a moment to understand his humor. "WAIT, we don't have anything to drink, he said, looking around the kitchen."

"Come with me," Anya said, taking Jacob by the hand. They walked down two hallways, eventually arriving at a nondescript door with an electronic keypad and a CCTV camera pod positioned just above the door frame. Anya pressed a series of five buttons and looked up into the camera. Moments later, the deadbolt in the door clicked loudly, and she opened the door, revealing a staircase descending just beyond the door. Jacob was intrigued by the facial recognition, all the security, and what Anya was about to show him. As they descended the metal staircase, motion detection lights activated, showing the few steps in front of them. They reached the bottom of the stairs as they rounded the corner, and Jacob was shocked. An underground cavern at least thirty feet wide by thirty long lay in front of them, filled with dusty bottles of wine.

Not your everyday liquor store wine selection, but expensive stuff, a 2010 DRC Domaine de la Romanée-Conti Richebourg Grand Cru, Chateau Lafite-Rothschild 2019, and dozens more with nothing under nine thousand dollars a bottle.

"Wonder where he keeps the beer," Jacob mumbled just loud enough for Anya to hear.

"In the Igloo cooler out by the outhouse," she said with a slight grin.

Jacob decided the best way to do this was by random selection, as he had no clue what any of these bottles tasted like. If it had been bottles of Scotch, maybe there would have been a better chance, but not here; this was way over the top for him. Jacob walked down the aisle and stopped, closed his eyes, and reached out to his right, grabbing the first bottleneck he felt. Removing it caused a small dust storm to swirl around. He used the sleeve of his shirt to remove the dust from the label. Handling the bottle to Anya, she was amused by Jacob's antics, as she examined the label.

"A 1981 Lafite Rothschild. It is good we drink this one now as it only has a few years left before you use it in spaghetti sauce," Anya turned and walked towards the stairs.

Jacob noticed scrape marks on the floor, a set of two. They were halfway down the aisle he was in and ended where a bottle shelf held several dozen dusty bottles of wine. He felt odd, as there was nothing nearby indicating that a heavy object had been brought to this area. However, the cement was clearly scraped recently.

Anya climbed the stairs, closing the door and confirming it was locked behind Jacob. The couple returned to the kitchen, and Jacob began cooking his meal fit for a bachelor. Anya opened the wine, pouring two glasses. Jacob took a sip and realized he did not have a palate for wine. The liquid was very good, but he realized that Anya could have slipped him a glass of Two Buck Chuck, and he would have never known the difference. He thought back to when he was just old enough to drink. His whiskey of choice was Jack Daniel's on the Rocks. One day, while he and his older brother Bryan were visiting their father, they were offered a glass of Jack Daniel's. As soon as Jacob tasted the brown liquid, he knew it was George Dickel's brand of whiskey. He had no complaints about this whiskey, which was one of the oldest and finest in Tennessee; however, he could taste the difference from Jack Daniel's, unlike his inability to taste the difference in the wine sitting in front of him. Anya was enjoying herself and was relaxed, as if she were at home in this mega-sized villa.

When the grilled cheese sandwiches with freshly cut tomatoes were on the table, the two sat and took their time eating and enjoying the wine. All was calm; they had a moment to breathe and think. Jacob ate quietly, looking down at his plate of food as Anya watched him, trying to figure out where his thoughts were.

"Agent Westerly, what are you thinking about?" Anya said calmly as Jacob looked up at her.

"It's Jacob Westerly. I think you can pretty much kiss my title and career goodbye. I don't know how I'm going to get out from under this. They have so much evidence that makes me look like a thief and a killer."

"I think the same people who tried to kill my father are also after you. They want to discredit you, make it so no one can trust you. But I can, I know you," Anya said sincerely, reaching over and taking Jacob's hand.

The quiet was disrupted by a cell phone ringing. Anya went to her bag and removed a small cell phone, pressing the button to answer. She spoke in her native language, which Jacob now recognized as a Central Russian dialect. During his time at FLETC, he learned some conversational Russian from a classmate, Nikolai, who had been born in the United States to Russian-Jewish parents. With Jacob's photographic memory, he found it easy to pick up language skills, even though Russian was one of the most challenging languages to learn. Nikolai would teach Jacob the words and sentence structure, and accompany him to building 75, where Jacob would make his food selection, telling Nikolai what he wanted in Russian, which Nikolai would then translate into English for the food server. He never told Anya about his skill, which allowed him an edge in times like this, as he sat drinking his wine as Anya spoke without concern.

The conversation was calm as Anya spoke in a low tone. Then, unexpectedly, her voice increased; the sound of her words was coming out as if she were winded and could not catch her breath. Jacob put his drink down and concentrated on Anya's behavior. She dropped her phone in distress, slumping down in the chair and softly crying. Jacob stood and sat on the arm of the chair with his hand on her back.

"What is it, Anya? What's wrong?"

"My father has just passed away. He did not make it out of the hospital," she said, sobbing.

"I'm so sorry," not knowing what else to say about the man who either planned or attempted Jacob's murder. Doing a football touchdown dance might not be appropriate right then. But thinking to himself, "There's more air to breathe now." Felt appropriate.

The two of them sat for several minutes, not speaking, only holding each other as Anya sat and cried. She eventually stopped, took a long, deep breath, and looked at Jacob.

"Those bastards in the Kremlin are responsible for this. They killed my father,"

"Why? How do you know this?" Jacob was curious about her assumption.

"They did not get the amount of money they expected from my father. Those bloodthirsty bastards,"

"What money? Why did your father owe the Kremlin money?"

"His ships. My father's oil companies had several ships that transported oil to other countries, thereby avoiding the sanctions. No one would touch him; he was safe. In exchange, he paid the old white-haired men in the Kremlin handsomely. They wanted more and he told them to fuck off. And then he decided to hurt the Kremlin. He developed a plan…" She stopped and thought for a moment, as if not sure whether to disclose these facts to Jacob. Jacob sat still, waiting to see what would come next.

Anya sat and for a moment reached down to pick up her phone. She dialed a number and began a conversation in Russian with the other person on the phone. Jacob could make out bits and pieces of what she was saying, something to indicate that it was time, they needed to talk with him, and when the caller would arrive. Jacob heard a series of words in Russian that he recognized.

"Я люблю тебя, дядя," (*I love you, uncle*) she said and disconnected the call.

Jacob tried to figure out his role in all this. He wanted to support Anya, but he also knew she wasn't telling him the whole truth.

"Who was that, Anya?" Hoping she would be truthful, but already knowing the answer.

"My Uncle Dmitri arrived at the hospital and found that my father had just died. He wants to come see me."

"When will he arrive?"

"In the next day or so, who knows. I never knew my father was that ill. I mean, he was sick, but I thought he was getting better; I guess I was wrong. Anya looked off in a daze. I think I will shower and go to bed."

"I understand. I'm going to sit up for a while and watch the local stations. Just to see what other lies are being said about me." Jacob sat on the overstuffed couch, looking at the remote control.

"Forget about the people who don't care about you. Remember those who do," Anya said as she kissed Jacob slowly and softly.

As Anya walked away toward the bedroom, Jacob sat looking at the screen of the 85-inch Samsung television, which was displayed in a way that made it almost appear to float. After about ten minutes of listening to Anya in the back room, Jacob quietly stood up and made his way down the hall. He paused at the bedroom door and glanced at his reflection in the mirror, where he could see Anya's naked body in the shower. Removing his sat phone from his pocket, he held the power button while pressing the number 5 key. This action activated a separate chip in the phone, which switched frequencies to a concealed number, allowing the caller to make calls or send texts.

The sat phone activated quickly, and a message indicated one text message waiting. Jacob pressed the receive button, and a photo of a three-headed dog statue appeared. The text message under the photo read, "dozens of these photos and statues in Nabil's apartment and on his laptop. Any clue?"

Jacob recognized the statue from Greek mythology; it was the watchdog of the underworld, Cerberus. Jacob typed in the name and hit send, then turned off the phone and placed it in his pocket. He could see Anya reach for a towel as she stepped out of the shower. Jacob walked back to the couch, taking his place where he had previously sat. Fumbling with the remote control, Jacob cycled through the various channels, making it seem like he was attempting to locate an English-speaking station.

Anya walked down the hall to say goodnight. She wore a full-length white terry cloth robe with white slippers, drying her hair as she approached Jacob. He paused his channel surfing and looked at Anya as he placed the remote on the couch and reached for her hand. Anya looked tired as she stepped across Jacob while he sat. Her naked body under the robe was slightly exposed as she straddled him and hugged him, her head resting on his shoulder. He slid his arms around her back beneath the robe as they lay there, comforting each other. The scent of her clean skin relaxed him, and he savored the moment. He could feel more than just his blood pressure beginning to rise, and when Anya sensed this, she slowly stood with her robe fully open.

"I'm sorry, my love. Not tonight. I just don't think I could. I hope you understand," she said, bending over to kiss him.

Jacob decided to take the high road and kissed her hand. "No problem, I understand. You go get yourself some sleep. I'll be there in a minute." Anya smiled and tied her robe closed before walking off. Jacob sat there, wondering if he would ever recover or if he would need a cold shower.

CHAPTER 16 (Say UNCLE)

As the morning sun began to rise, Jacob reflected on what would come in the near-distant future. Anya's Uncle Dmitri Stanislavski was due to arrive shortly, and Jacob was not sure how this spymaster would feel about a disgraced U.S. Federal Agent. Jacob was familiar with Anya's family background, having researched it while at FLETC. Stone had given Jacob a dossier on Anya as a welcoming gift to the unit. He felt that his new recruit should know how the Russian spy groups worked and that they had used Jacob's relationship with Anya for their own gain. Research is what Jacob liked to do, on any topic. But when it came to a person who tried to kill him, he wanted to know everything.

The Stanislavski family had a rich history, dating back to the 1300s. Peter, whose legal name was Pyotr, and his younger brother Dmitri were brought up in a family that was close to Tsar Nicholas II until Vladimir Lenin replaced him in 1917. At that time, they found favor with Lenin by owning an interest in factories and land, which they could farm as nobles or use as politicians. Their wealth grew quickly, and so did their political might. The Stanislavski family positioned themselves in 1999 when Vladimir Putin became President, and the family opened the oil fields in Siberia to foreign exploration first, then took over the job and retained the profits for themselves. Several family offshoots were part of the People's Commissariat for Internal Affairs (NKVD), which served as the foundation for the KGB. It was the law enforcement arm of the Communist Party and began honing its spy skills, eventually being known as the Soviet Secret Police.

Jacob knew that Anya's family had one goal: to keep the money in the family at any cost. They had plenty of money, which was used around the world to buy politicians and police, hire assassins, and enjoy the benefits that come with having endless dollars in the bank. However, they had recently fallen out of favor with the Kremlin for reasons that were not entirely clear. Anya's hint that her father was not making payments could have offered a vague glimpse into the family's operations, but more information was needed. Normally, the CIA would take the lead in these matters; however, with Jacob being framed for murder and theft, he was unsure whom to trust in his government. He felt like he was on an island, with hungry sharks just off the beach.

Would Dmitri provide a way off the island or throw Jacob to the sharks for a fee? Jacob checked his phone; the time was 5:05 am, time for a couple more hours of sleep.

It was the smell that awoke him. Cologne. His eyes were still closed as he tried to figure out if Anya was wearing something different than the perfume he was accustomed to. He took a deep breath and opened his eyes.

"Wholly shit," Jacob blurted out.

Jacob reached for the table next to him, where he had left his Glock G43 9mm automatic handgun under a magazine he had been reading before falling asleep. However, both the magazine and his gun were missing. He noticed a bald-headed man sitting in a chair just a foot from the side of his bed, seemingly analyzing Jacob as he slept.

"It's okay, Jacob. You do not need a gun," the man said in a deep Russian accent as he stood.

Anya also awoke and turned to see the man, accompanied by several other men dressed in suits, standing around the room watching.

"Uncle Dmitri!" Anya yelled as she jumped out of bed naked. The five men around the room, seeing the woman unclothed, made a point of averting their attention so as not to offend the man in the chair. Anya grabbed her robe off the bed, tying the garment shut as she hugged the man. Jacob sat up in bed, unsure of what to do as he watched the men, who had obvious weapons protruding from the front openings in their suits.

"I am so glad you made it here. I was not sure when you would arrive."

The man started to reply in Russian at which time Anya stopped him.

"Please, Uncle, English. I want to introduce you to someone very special…"

"Yes, Jacob Westerly, we just met. As I am sure you know, I am Anastasia's Uncle, Dmitri Stanislavski. I have heard many wonderful things about you, young man," Dmitri said as he extended his hand to Jacob.

"Uh, thank you, sir. It's a pleasure," Jacob said, slightly guarded. Not sure how he should behave, looking around the room, trying to establish where his gun might be.

Dmitri turned his attention back to Anya.

"I am so sorry about your father, my brother. He will be missed. The doctors told me that he died quickly, with no pain. He used to be known as The Eagle," he said in a low tone, a reference to Prince Pyotr Bagration in Leo Tolstoy's War and Peace.

"Yes, I heard that title several times while growing up. I thought he was getting better; this was such a shock. You know who is responsible for this, yes?" Anya's voice had a hint of anger.

"They will pay for it in time, I assure you," Dmitri said, holding his hands on each shoulder. "I need some coffee, and Bobby, you need to give Jacob his gun back. He feels naked without it." He turned his attention to one of the men standing around the room and laughed.

The man removed the Glock from his waistband, released the magazine, and racked the slide to eject the single round, which flew past them and landed on the bed. He then slowly raised the gun, pointing it at Jacob's head with a grin on his face, before releasing his grip, but keeping his index finger inside the trigger guard as the gun spun. Finally, he extended the weapon toward Jacob. Slowly, Jacob took the gun and magazine as the men followed Anya and Dmitri out of the room. "Message received," Jacob thought to himself.

The group gathered in Dmitri's spacious kitchen, savoring coffee and fresh pastries from the village bakery. A guard for Dmitri stood at the stove, wearing an apron over his shoulder holster containing a Beretta 92 Combat 9-millimeter semi-automatic handgun. As the armed cook finished an omelet, he would place it on the cutting board, slice it into strips, then move it to a serving plate on the large granite island where the men and Anya sat sipping coffee and indulging in pastries and eggs as they talked. Jacob did more listening than talking, as most of the conversation was in Russian.

"Jacob, when did you know that Anya filled your heart?" Dmitri said.

"Uncle, don't put him on the spot, you old romantic," Anya said as she glanced at Jacob's direction.

"No, it's okay. I remember the exact moment even today," Jacob said, finishing his cup of coffee.

"Please, tell us. We all love a great love story," Dmitri proclaimed as he lifted his coffee cup to salute.

"It was in March, a Saturday?" Jacob looked at Anya inquisitively. She nodded and smiled. "We were both at a cocktail party for a local newspaper that my," Jacob paused for a moment, thinking, then continued. "I was at the bar trying to decide a drink to have, and your niece told the bartender to make me a…" He searched for his words as he looked at Anya, confused.

"Seedlip," Anya said.

"Yes, Seedlip with ginger ale. I turned, and there was the most beautiful woman I had ever seen. I think I spent five minutes looking at her green eyes and having no words come from my mouth," Jacob looked at Dmitri, who had a look for approval, nodding his head yes. The other men in the room did not smile and looked at Jacob as if they could pull their guns and fill him with holes, and then finish their coffee.

"Anastasia, did you feel this also?" Dmitri queried Anya across the island.

"No," as everyone looked up at Anya. The men smiled and Dmitri looked confused. "I knew it as I saw this young handsome man standing at the bar like a boy ordering a 'cocktail'."

The men lost their smiles, realizing Anya had an attraction for this foreigner whom they did not trust. One of the men grumbled, saying something in Russian under his breath that everyone could hear. Anya turned to the man, speaking to him in a single sentence in Russian that he understood, without choosing to say anything further. The other men laughed out loud as the man sulked and looked down at his cup of coffee angrily.

"This is our guest. You will treat him with respect, or I will let my niece have her way with you," Dmitri's statement caused the men to moan with approval, as Anya took a large knife from the block, slamming it down point first on the cutting board, so it remained stuck with the handle upwards. Anya made a childish smile at the man who had made the disparaging remark. He understood, as did Jacob, who was not smiling and looking around, evaluating the laughing men in front of him.

"Jacob, let us take our coffee on the balcony and talk," Dmitri said, picking up his cup as one of the men topped it off with coffee. Jacob looked around, realizing no one was moving to fill his half-empty cup. He reached over, only to have one of the men grab the decanter and pour the last of the coffee into his own cup, as he smiled at Jacob.

Jacob stood and followed Dmitri onto the balcony. One of his men stood near the window, keeping an eye on the American lawman. Looking out over the balcony railing, Dmitri sighed.

"Anastasia told me about the problems you are having with the American Government. It sounds bad. It sounds like they have, uh, how do you say, hung you out to dry. I have checked with my contacts in the Department of Justice, and they say you are being used as a scapegoat. They have no intention of bringing you back in any honorable way. They plan to convict you and put you in the same facility Anastasia was in, as a traitor."

Jacob dropped his head, shaking it. "Damn it," he said just loud enough to make sure Dmitri could hear.

"Your goose is cooked, Mr. Westerly. Even if you were to return and fight these charges and win, you would always be looked upon as the traitor who won. Of course, you and my niece could run, and hide in countries that do not care about your charges, but that would mean no contact at all with your family. Any phone call would mean your location was known, and your black ops people would hunt you down. And even when you put your hands up to surrender, well, their story would be that you resisted. And goodbye, former traitor Jacob Westerly."

Jacob sat quietly, looking out over the vineyard as the sun grew stronger and the day warmed. Dmitri sipped his coffee, letting his words sink in. Anya stepped out onto the balcony with a fresh coffee press, filling Jacob's cup and then her uncle's. Dmitri gave her a gentle, affectionate kiss on the cheek.

"I know all is feeling lost; however, we, I mean my uncle, can fix this. We can make you whole again. There is a way to change the narrative and show your innocence from the highest level," Anya said softly.

Jacob looked up and then turned. He was interested and wanted to hear more. Placing his coffee cup on the railing, his face showed concern.

"How? How is this possible? They have so much manufactured evidence against me. There is no way I could explain this."

"You do not need to explain anything. You simply help us and we help you," Anya explained.

"How can I help you? What could I possibly do?"

"Occasionally, information crosses your desk and needs to find its way to us. That's all," Dmitri explained.

"What? Give you information? That would make me a spy," Jacob said, concerned.

"Right now, Jacob, you are a traitor in the eyes of your country. If you are lucky, if…you will be arrested and make it home alive. That is, if no one kills you while you wait for your trial. Hopefully, when they arrest you, there will be many news cameras on you to prevent an accidental killing of you. But I sincerely doubt it. With us, we can return you to your old life, just as if none of this had happened. Like a time machine of sorts. You would live a long and fulfilling life, perhaps even retiring from the government to collect your modest retirement benefits. And did I mention you would be paid handsomely for your loyalty?" Dmitri made it all sound so easy.

"Just information. No killings or sabotage or anything like that?" Jacob asked.

"Please Mr. Westerly, we are not killers, just opportunists, like that bastard in the Kremlin."

Jacob walked to the end of the balcony alone, as if considering his options. Then he returned to Anya and Dmitri.

"Would we be together?" he said looking at Anya.

Stepping close to Anya, she gave Jacob a kiss and a soft hug. Dmitri smiled, and he put his hand on Jacob's shoulder.

"Okay. I have nothing else to lose, so why not? My people have obviously done nothing to help me, and you have," Jacob said, reaching out to shake Dmitri's hand.

"Wonderful. Do not worry, our family has been doing this for centuries. Just stay loyal and avoid getting greedy. Let's go inside and let the other know."

The three of them walked into the room, where the suited men were sitting on stools, still eating and drinking coffee. A bottle of vodka was on the counter.

"Новый член семьи (*New family member*)," Dmitri said as he placed his arm around Jacob's shoulder. The men cheered as they lifted their mugs, and some took shots of vodka to celebrate the announcement.

Anya looked over at Dmitri and said something in Russian under her breath. He smiled and shook his head.

"Young man, we have something to show you that might explain more. Follow me," Dmitri and Anya said, walking off with Jacob close behind.

Walking down the hallway to the door that Anya and Jacob had previously entered the wine cellar, Dmitri punched in a series of numbers on the keypad and then looked at the camera. Once again, the sound of a deadbolt opening shook the wall as Dmitri unlocked the door, and Anya descended the stairs with Jacob close behind. Walking to the end of the wine cellar where Jacob had previously looked at the scrape marks on the cement floor, Anya stopped. She looked up and examined the bottles, reaching up to touch one, but nothing happened. Dmitri stepped around her.

"Anastasia, you can never seem to remember our favorite wine," he said, touching a bottle three over to the left of Anya's.

Moments later, an overhead light turned on, illuminating the wall as the entire shelf appeared to release, slightly coming forward. With one hand, Anya opened the shelf as if it were a door on a smooth gliding hinge, revealing a dark room behind the newly opened door.

Dmitri walked in as a dozen automatic lights activated, exposing a room much larger than the wine cellar behind him. Dozens of wooden boxes lay stacked atop each other, with beige climate-controlled cabinets in a line against one of the walls. The room sloped slightly downward, with the end projecting slightly to the right, out of sight. Jacob stood silently, observing and looking around. His photographic memory came into play as it recorded boxes and numbers written in Russian, painted on each faceplate.

Anya walked to a beige drawer, reaching on top where a wooden box rested, she removed a pair of white cotton gloves, placing them on her hands. Taking hold of the beige drawer in hand and opening it, a whoosh of air could be heard, signaling the climate control system was on pause. Reaching into the drawer, Anya removed a black chalice, carefully placing it on the table next to her.

"Do you know what this is?" she asked Jacob.

"No. A vase?" trying to sound intelligent.

"No, my love, this is a chalice. One was made for the Knights Templar out of obsidian. A wealthy Russian businessman owned it until the French Government seized it. And then we seized it." Anya gently placed the black chalice into the drawer, closing it.

Walking over to a large wooden box, Anya unlatched the front and gently lowered the door. This exposed a painting wrapped in soft linen. She stepped back, admiring the painting.

"You have to love a van Gogh. This is one of my favorites: Still Life, Vase with Daisies, and Poppies. Vincent van Gogh died in 1890, and this painting of his was sold in 1911 to a Berlin Art dealer, who loaned it to the Albright-Knox Art Gallery. The owner then sold it. Eventually, that owner sold it at Sotheby's for $61 million to a wealthy Russian who lost it to the Italian Government, and here it sits, in our collection." She said, smiling.

Behind that painting, Anya produced another, Rembrandt's Christ in the Storm on the Sea of Galilee, stolen in March 1990 from the Isabella Stewart Gardner Museum in Boston. Holding the two paintings side by side, she acted confused. The painting illustrates the moment when Jesus Christ and his disciples encounter a violent storm while crossing the Sea of Galilee.

"I am not sure which is my favorite, van Gogh or Rembrandt. They both would look good in my living room, but then people would talk and bring unwanted attention."

The three walked around the corner to a large rolling door. She removed her white gloves and threw them on the floor. Dmitri shook his head and reached down, picking them up, placing the gloves in his pocket. Anya pressed a large, yellow button that slowly opened the door, which resembled a nuclear blast door. The room inside was breathtaking. The sheer size was unimaginable. The villa sitting above the enclosure must have been the size of a fly upon an elephant's back. The ground is smooth cement, with yellow lines designating the parking spots for the vehicles contained inside.

In Jacob's first year as a multi-millionaire, he became obsessed with finding a car that no one else would have. He dreamed of driving down the freeway, with everyone fixing their gaze on his unique car. It may have been vain, but it was a common occurrence among young people who inherited vast wealth without a proper family background and upbringing.

To Anya, cars were simply machines that got you from point A to point B in comfort. To Jacob, they were a symbol of wealth, a status symbol of someone who had obtained riches because good fortune had smiled upon them. He began to walk slowly through the cavern, taking note of the motorized art in front of him.

De Tomaso P72 1.3 million, McLaren Elva 1.7 million, Aston Martin Vulcan 2.3 million, Bugatti Centodieci 9 million, and it went on and on. Jacob turned and looked at Anya and Dimitri, who were watching him.

A bottle sitting on a wooden crate, out of view, intrigued Jacob. His guests watched him as he slowly made his way to the bottle, lifting it and taking time to examine the wording on the label.

"Glenlochy Scotch, 1926," carefully moving the bottle as if filled with nitroglycerin.

"You know your whiskeys, Jacob. Very impressive. Only 100 bottles were produced before the distillery closed in 1983. That particular bottle was purchased at auction for $2.7 million. Would you care to taste it?" Dimitri said with a tone of amusement in his voice.

"Where did all these come from?" Jacob asked.

"Courtesy of your government. Rich Oligarchs owned them, then your people owned them, and then we stole them, simple," Anya said, tilting her head and smiling.

"And you just keep them here? That's it? And how did you know where to locate them?" Questions ran through his head and came out of his mouth in no specific order.

"This is, as you say, the tip of the ice cube," Anya said

"Iceberg, the tip of the iceberg," Jacob corrected her.

"Oh, there you go again with the corrections. Can't you let me have my hour?"

He was about to correct that statement but thought he might be pushing his luck. After all, he was the new kid on the block and needed to get any information possible.

Like a Racoon attracted to a shiny object, Jacob turned his attention to a round metal canister the size of a 50-gallon drum sitting in the corner of the room. The top of the canister was half-round and secured with several bands, each holding a long rod to the top. A digital numbering device was attached with a small LCD screen that glowed red.

Dimitri observed Jacob's interest in the canister and stepped up to his side, looking in the same direction.

"Interesting, isn't it?" Dimitri asked.

"Whatever is inside is meant to stay inside. What does it hold, the Crown Jewels?" Jacob asked sarcastically.

"No, no. The Crown Jewels were taken years ago; the ones you see now are fakes," he laughed slightly. Jacob turned his attention to Dimitri.

"Fakes? You have the real ones?"

"Yes," he said with a laugh. They are here somewhere, perhaps with the Holy Grail. No one is sure, so much stuff," waving his hand and giving Jacob a wink.

Jacob could not tell if he was joking or blowing him off, so the questions would stop.

Pointing at the canaster, "Now that young man is from an era long before your time. When my country and yours believed we would both end the world at the push of a button. Fortunately, your President Kennedy had, uh, what do you say? Brass Balls, and he convinced our leadership that he was serious if we kept playing around in Cuba. He made a deal with us so his fighter jets would not have to start a quick and possibly very short World War Three."

"The Cuban Missile Crisis? I read about that," Jacob recalled to Dimitri.

"What your newspapers did not say was how much uranium-237 had been collected and was on warheads, ready to visit your country. Once the Cold War ended and missiles were dismantled, the Uranium needed a home. And now we have given it one, which will soon be purchased by North Korea. As for all the rest of these items, we have buyers all over the world," he explained.

"You can't exactly put these things on Craigslist and sell them. How do you get rid of them?"

"The previous owners are unhappy that government officials removed these from their homes. They have wives, girlfriends, and mistresses who enjoy their toys. Some want them back, while others want them sold. If we sell them, the previous owner gets a percentage back," Anya explained.

"Where did you find these?" prodding for more answers.

"We have people all over the world who have access to the lists of seized Russian goods and where they are kept. Many of the people in the Ukrainian Asset and Recovery Management Agency work for us. You would be amazed at what a little money can buy. We also have over two dozen mega yachts, like my beloved Anastasia Dream. Unfortunately, it is in the hands of the man you sold it to, and I would no longer be able to enjoy it if we removed it from his dock."

"Yeah, it has some bad memories for me too," Jacob said to Anya.

"Do you have some big cave somewhere like this one where you keep the ships?"

"No, no, Jacob, they are repainted, fitted with new AIS systems, and hidden in places where satellites will not look for them, like the Amazon or deep in rivers of Russia. And, of course, we have people who obtain the satellite images, working for your government, who alter them and make sure analysts do not find our treasures," Dmitri explained.

"Why is the Kremlin so pissed at you guys?"

"Not you guys, us! Remember, you are now part of us." Anya reminded Jacob.

"Yes, sorry, us!"

"The fat boy Oligarchs are not happy that the Kremlin is no longer protecting them, and then, on top of it all, my brother stopped giving them a percentage of the oil profits from his Dark Fleet deliveries. They need this money for the war effort. Soon, the people of Russia will grow tired of the war, and the "boss" will be no more. Then we will all return to our regular day jobs, as you might say," Dmitri smiled.

"Where do I fit in? What do you want from me?"

"Like we said, my dear boy, information. Just information. You will return to work shortly, and everyone will be told this was a big mistake. My people are working on it as I speak. I understand you have an important historical document that the Italians were interested in. May I see it?" Dmitri asked.

"Yes, sir, it's up in my bag."

Dmitri motioned for Jacob to lead the way back. They closed the doors behind them and returned to the upstairs living area, where the guards were sitting and watching a soccer game on the television. Jacob walked into the bedroom, picked up his bag, and then returned to the living room.

Jacob removed the document, which was contained in a plastic protective wrap. Dmitri took the white cotton gloves from his pocket that he had picked up from the floor and carefully slipped them onto each hand. He took great care in handling the document, placing it on a cloth on the table. Jacob watched closely to see the man's reaction and if he could authenticate it. Dmitri took a small examining glass from his pocket and pressed it to his right eye, holding it in place. He gently lifted the document and studied the words closely.

"Mussolini was an idiot, thinking he could win Hitler over with a piece of land," he said in a low voice. "Why was this so important to you that deceiving the Italian Interpol was required?

"At the time, I was unaware of your group and its purpose. I wiped the document and analyzed any touch DNA found. Everyone who previously handled this document wore cotton gloves, except one person," Jacob explained.

"Do you know who that person is?" Dmitri's face was no longer smiling, he was very serious and to the point."

"No, it was too degraded to be useful," hoping his answer sounded believable.

CHAPTER 17 (Change in Plans)

Master Sergeant Chuck Hoover was so focused on the browser of his cell phone that he paid little attention to the staff in the Load Control Office at Ramstein Air Force Base, Germany. He was determined to find the perfect house to purchase for his fiancée, Natalia. Chuck and Natalia met one night at a bar just outside the Base. Although Chuck was still married to Lucy back in the States, he couldn't help but be attracted to the beautiful blonde who accidentally backed into him while playing pool. She was a bit drunk with her group of friends who were out celebrating her new job as a makeup artist. The Tree Bar #3 was a popular hangout for off-duty military personnel and a nice place to meet up with friends for the night. Chuck spent nearly an hour after their meet-cute with Natalia as they continued their conversation at a separate pool table and then moved to their own table, ignoring the company they had arrived with.

Natalia was flirtatious yet guarded when Chuck suggested they meet again for drinks or that she could show him around the area on his days off. Initially, Natalia hesitated to give him her cell number, but he countered by offering his instead. She accepted, and everything fell into place. As the days turned into weeks, they spent every moment together when Chuck was not on base.

Eventually, they made their way to Natalia's apartment, a cute little single room in the town of Landstuhl. The apartment was nicely decorated and comfortable. Natalia loved having a 55-inch TV mounted on her wall. They would sit on the couch for hours, watching shows and sporting events. That time on the couch eventually turned into an intimate location, where the attention to the television was replaced with the removal of clothes. Frequently, Natalia would express her concern that Chuck was married and she was just "the other woman" in his life.

"Natalia, that's not true. You know how I feel about you. Lucy just doesn't understand me. She's so cold, and I'm the one who has to initiate phone calls or Zoom chats. I really don't see how my marriage can last much longer," Chuck would say in a sad voice, causing Natalia to take him in her arms and comfort him, which led to more sex and more.

Their romance grew stronger with each passing week. On a Saturday afternoon, while hiking in the hills near Fleischackerloch Landstuhl, they paused and sat on a large rock, resting and drinking some water. Chuck unzipped his backpack and got up, turning to face Natalia.

Attempting to kneel, he lost his balance and stumbled to the ground. Natalia, rushing to break his fall, ended up lying on the ground laughing as she looked at him curiously. Leaves in their hair, looking totally disheveled.

"Chuck, what was that all about?" she said, giggling.

Gaining his composure and trying to look serious, he slowly knelt on one knee, holding out a small ring box, which he opened, displaying a gold band with a small diamond mounted in the center.

"Natalia, I know we've only been together for a couple of months, but this time with you makes me think about nothing other than us. I understand you are concerned about my marriage to Lucy, and I have decided to file for divorce this month when I return to the States on leave. With that in mind, when I'm free from this nightmare, would you consider marrying me? Forever?" as he removed the ring from the box.

Natalia sat looking at the ring and then at Chuck, her mouth slightly open in a display of shock. Slowly, her face turned to elation as her breathing increased.

"Yes, yes, of course, I will, Chuck. Oh my God, I cannot believe this?"

She reached out with both hands to Chuck's face and kissed him, almost knocking the box out of his hand. His quick reaction caught the box, and he removed the ring and placed it on Natalia's finger. Unbeknownst to the couple, several hikers had seen the proposal and began clapping. Chuck gave Natalia a long kiss, pausing to look at her and smile.

It was a beautiful, clear day with temperatures in the mid-sixties; while Chuck was eating lunch by himself at a fast-food restaurant off base, he was enjoying his hamburger when his phone buzzed, signaling that an email had arrived. The email was from someone he did not recognize, and upon opening the email, he sat staring at the screen in disbelief. There was a photo of him in Natalia's apartment, naked, along with Natalia. The photo was of them having sex on the couch with Natalia in a very compromising position. The following four photos appeared after this, which were more similar but in very graphic positions at different times and places.

Chuck could feel his heart racing and sweat coming from every part of his body. His mind was racing as he thought about what these photos could do to him if others ever saw them in his family, and worse, the Military.

"What the fuck?" Chuck kept repeating.

"Excuse me, Master Sergeant Chuck Hoover?" the man standing before his table asked.

Chuck froze. Was this the FBI or the OSI (Office of Special Investigations)? Were they contacting him about the photos? Then anger washed over him. Why him? Who was doing this?

"Who the fuck are you?" just came blurting out, even surprising Chuck.

The man paused, just looking at Chuck without emotion.

"I'm the guy who can make all those photos go away and make you whole again," he spoke in a serious tone.

Chuck had yet to see the second man standing directly to his right, slightly behind where Chuck was seated. Until he attempted to stand. A hand was placed on his right shoulder, and he was gently seated back in front of his hamburger and fries. Chuck decided not to resist whoever these two were.

The man slid into the booth directly across from Chuck. He picked up a cold fry and took a bite. His face was wincing.

"I never could understand what Americans and British find so intriguing about fried potatoes," dropping the fry on the table and returning his attention to the man sweating in front of him. "Those are some very nasty photographs, Staff Sergeant. And especially for a married man. Do you think Lucy would be interested in these?"

"Who are you? What do you want with me? Are you related to her?" Chuck was firing off questions as quickly as his brain created the thought.

"Relax, Sergeant. She is just an employee."

"Employee for who?" and then it hit him. He was being compromised. Probably by a foreign Government. He recalled in his training that this is how assets are created, and now they were looking at him.

"Those photos don't matter to me. After all, I'm about to file for divorce in a no-fault state. So what?" he was feeling pretty confident in this game of chess… checkmate, he thought.

"Let's just cut through the crap. These photos will end your marriage, your security clearance, and most likely, your career. Along with any retirement you expect to receive," the man said, with Chuck beginning to think more of the ramifications of his actions.

"What if I go to the authorities first and explain all of this?" he tried to counter.

"Sure, contact your FBI or OSI and be a hero. But it still doesn't change the photos and what they show. Oh, and did I mention that we created an offshore account in your name? One that has been receiving five-thousand-dollar payments for the last several months? And that eight-thousand-dollar credit card bill, you have been worried about? Paid in full a few days ago from that special account you failed to tell anyone about. And let's not forget that both your and Lucy's signatures are on the documents. What do you think she will say when the FBI shows up at your home in Michigan asking about that? Lucy, you got some splain ta do!" the man chuckled as his eyebrows raised.

"What do you want?" an exhausted and beaten-down Air Force Sergeant said in a low voice.

"Nothing. Every so often, a special manifest will come to you for the items we need to be moved, and you will simply approve it and let it proceed, just like the hundreds you process each week. We find that the United States Military Airlift Command can be trusted to get our cargo to its destination better than your Postal Services," he laughed lightly while watching Chuck's response.

"And that's it? Nothing else?"

"That's it. Of course, you will be provided with the offshore account information and will be handsomely paid for your loyalty. This is just a small way we say thanks," the man said, rising from his seat.

As the men left, Master Sergeant Chuck Hoover remained seated in front of his cold hamburger, staring out the window, taking in what had just happened. Then a thought came to him: He needed to go to the apartment and find Natalia.

Twenty minutes later, he arrived at the apartment and made his way to the front door. He found it open, with two apartment employees steam-cleaning the rugs. The apartment was absent of any belongings that were present 24 hours prior. A short walk put him at the apartment manager's office. He entered and found a middle-aged woman seated behind the desk.

"May I help you, sir?" She asked, smiling.

"The young lady in apartment G201 appears not to be living there. I have a book I was returning, and it surprised me that she was gone. Can you tell me if she provided a forwarding address?" He paused, holding up the hardback book he had removed from his car.

"No, she did not. An envelope with her key and some cash was dropped through the door last night. Miss Hoover was a wonderful tenant. Maybe if you know any of her friends, they can give you more information," she suggested.

"Miss Hoover? Are you sure we are talking about the same person?"

The woman opened a file, taking a moment to scan the document.

"Yes, Lucy Hoover. She had just come for a few months from Lansing, Michigan," she said, looking up at the man in front of her, who appeared to be in a daze.

Lucy Hoover from Lansing, Michigan. They used his wife's name and hometown, which he kept thinking over and over. Chuck slowly turned and walked out of the office.

Stone parked his car in a nondescript lot adjacent to the Ramstein Air Base. The guards at the front gate were expecting his arrival and cleared his entry once he showed his Justice Department credentials. As he walked up to the massive rolling gate separating him from the airfield, he noticed no security or personnel present. A woman wearing an olive-green jumpsuit stood on the airfield, checking her cell phone. Stone stopped and stood at the gate, not making a sound as he kept his attention on the lone airman. Military aircraft taxied slowly to their runways while others roared by, making any noise hard to hear. The airman looked up briefly and noticed Stone standing at the gate. She walked towards him, sliding her cell phone into the upper pocket of her jumpsuit, just above her left elbow.

"Agent Stone?" she asked.

Stone nodded as the woman waved her hand and the large fence came to life, slowly opening. Stone walked in as the airman approached.

"I'm Senior Airman Donna Walters, loadmaster on the C-130 that will take you back to the States. Do you have any other luggage, sir?"

"Just this," Stone lifted his attaché containing his electronic notepad.

"Very good, right this way, sir," Walters walked away from the fence with Stone beside her. In front of them was a massive C-130 Hercules J-Model.

Stone looked at the tail and noted its number, 20-5945. As the runway sound subsided, Stone yelled at the young airman.

"Where's the plane based?"

"We're part of the Kentucky Air National Guard, 123rd Airlift Wing, sir."

"Where are we headed?"

"Joint Base Andrews, sir," as they approached the C-130 with its rear door open.

Stone followed Walters up the plane's rear ramp. With the exception of one small crate, the plane was empty. Walters pulled down a red mesh seat from the side of the aircraft and loosened the shoulder belts on the wall.

"This will be home for the next nine hours, sir. We have some food and water for the trip, and if you need the head, it's located here. Walters walked over to the rear side of the aircraft, where the rear ramp was hinged. A small toilet was mounted above a box. Walters pulled the curtain back, holding it with the strap.

"First-class accommodations, sir." She smiled at Stone. "Wheels up in ten minutes, get comfortable. Here is a headset to communicate with the crew during the flight. It also works great as an ear muff if you want to catch some sleep." She handed the headset to Stone and pointed to a wall jack he could plug into.

Stone settled in as the C-130 taxied to the end of the runway, slowly gaining power with its four Rolls-Royce Allison AE 2100D3 turboprops. The headsets muted the hum inside the plane as it lifted off, banking steeply and then slowly leveling off. Opening his attaché, Stone removed his tablet and turned it on. He opened the first folder of photographs and documents. The password request box opened, and Stone typed in the newly discovered word, provided by Jacob. The photos opened one by one across the screen. Stone then accessed a PDF document and reviewed the spreadsheet of names, dates of enlistment, spouses' names, and addresses. American law enforcement agents, police officers, and even local motor vehicle department employees were listed. The scale of infiltration was immense and impressive. How could so many people become involved with an organization that our country has always been suspicious of? If this had been a list of U.S. assets in a hostile country, these people would have been arrested and assassinated one by one until the list was clear. Thankfully, the worst these people would get is jail time. Once discovered, countless careers, lives, and marriages would be ruined by greed, he thought.

Opening the next document revealed a list of tanker ships, their names, captains, location of origin, and dated destinations. The Dark Fleet, he thought. These were ships that became untouchable. Only by luck would a Military ship spot them on the high seas and attempt to stop and board them. Countries such as India and Iran permitted the ships to unload their oil, if they made it, slowing the sanction efforts of the allies. Was this why Bennett recalled Stone back to the States, or did it have to do with Westerly?

As Stone scanned the photos, he stopped on one in particular. Interesting he thought. Just then, the door to the cockpit closed, drawing Stone's attention to the pilot walking towards him. Stone stood to meet him.

"Agent Stone, I'm Captain Bill Hickock, and no, they don't call me wild Bill; that's for the fighter pilots," he smiled and extended his hand to Stone.

"Nice to meet you, Captain, what can I do for you?"

"I just received an update on your trip. This is really strange Agent Stone, and frankly hard to wrap my head around, but orders are orders," he said as he sat and invited Stone to do the same.

Stone was interested in the idea that the pilot himself would come back to update Stone. Bad weather? Mechanical issue? The thoughts just kept coming.

"I have been ordered to fly you to the Duluth-based Air National Guard unit and not allow you off the plane until we enter a secure hanger," he said, waiting to see what the Agent in front of him would do.

"OK, is there any explanation for these orders?"

"In my 25 years of military service, I have never received orders directly from the SecDef (Secretary of Defense) that were from the White House, actually my Commander in Chief, until now. We have been instructed by MCON (Mission Control) to turn off our transponder system and go completely dark. This is normally done in combat areas, but the last time I checked, there was no war in Minnesota. I checked with a buddy of mine in the FAA, and he told me that the orders were correct, and his unit had been instructed not to discuss or intercept this aircraft," the captain explained.

"Why would they intercept one of their own planes?"

"NORAD (North American Aerospace Defense Command) monitors anyone flying into U.S. or Canadian airspace from 700 miles out. If we were not squawking with ground control, fighters would be scrambled to intercept us and identify if we were friend or foe. This won't happen,"

"Well, this is unusual, and you say it came from the White House? Should I consider myself under arrest?" Stone asked with concern.

"That was never mentioned. This order came directly from the President, sir. Agent Stone, can I ask what this is all about, or is it beyond my security clearance?"

"I'm not sure what I can tell you, or if knowing something could put you at risk."

"Is there anything I need to know that might risk the safety of this plane or my crew? That, Agent Stone, I do have a need to know," the captain was trying to show Stone how serious he was about this statement.

"No, sir. I have nothing but documents on me and, of course, my duty weapon, but that's all," Stone opened the right side of his jacket in an attempt to put the captain's mind at ease. "Is there any issue with me being armed on this flight?"

"No, sir. We fly transport. That includes the CIA, Troops, and Snake Eaters, they're all armed to the teeth."

"Snake Eaters?" Stone asked inquisitively.

"Special Forces guys, you know the ones who live in the jungles and have to survive on minimal supplies. It's an old term that came from the Vietnam era, still used today," the captain explained.

"When we arrive, if there is an order for me to come out and surrender for any reason, I will be unarmed, I'll surrender my weapon to you."

"I get the feeling it's nothing like that. Why they would have me go dark, when satellites can still track me, is a question that keeps running through my head. They don't want others, whoever those others are, to know where we land. I'll keep you updated if I learn more," he said and began to walk off.

"Captain, I noticed this was the only cargo you had," referring to the four-foot by four-foot wooden crate tied down in front of him. "Do you know its source?"

"No, sir," Airman Walters said, she reviewed the manifest, signed by Master Sergeant Hoover on his electronic notepad. "My notes say you requested it be loaded for the trip back," he said, looking at Stone, who was showing concern.

"Captain, are you at cruising altitude?"

"No sir, we should be at thirty thousand feet in a few minutes, why?"

"Drop your cargo door and jettison this. I think it contains explosives,"

With that statement, the captain immediately grabbed the mic on the wall and ordered the loadmaster to the cargo bay.

Airman Walter opened the forward door and ran back to the captain's location.

"Oxygen masks on and jettison this crate, it has explosives inside," the captain yelled.

"Captain, this box is not weighted for dropping," Walters explained.

"Are you going to get rid of this box or not?" Stone asked.

"It's not that easy. Cargo that's dropped from these planes are carefully weighted down so the updraft coming from the plane does lift them and damage the tail,"

"I can rig up a slingshot and tie on one of the sandbags I have up front along with several dead weights that the Special Ops guys use to work out with on long flights. That should get the crate out far enough that any upward lift will clear the tail," Walters said.

"Do it, fast!" the captain ordered.

Reaching between Stone's seat, the pilot pulled down a hinged rectangle plastic door on the wall. Inside, two oxygen masks and ten-foot hoses connected to the aircraft were stored.

Handing a mask to Stone, who held it against his face as he pulled the straps back behind his head, securing the mask in place.

Picking up the wall mic, Hickcock notified the co-pilot and crew up front to hold their altitude and put on oxygen masks.

The loadmaster rigged up several ropes secured to black sandbags and dead weights. A long bungee-style cord was hooked onto specially fitted tracks in the middle of the floor, allowing the wooden crate to slide out the back door when opened. She put on her helmet and face mask, activating the portable oxygen tank attached to her.

"Let me know when we are feet wet," Hickcock instructed the flight deck. This indicated that they had cleared European airspace and were flying over the North Sea.

The flight deck indicated all was ready to open the rear cargo door. With everyone in the back securely tethered, Walters pressed a control button that slowly opened the door. The rush of cold air and drop in pressure momentarily shocked Stone as he held firmly to his chair frame. With a push, Walters and Hickock released the tie-down straps around the crate and sent it rolling out the back door, dropping behind the plane. The three of them watched as moments before the crate struck the water, it exploded into a fiery ball. They looked at each other, their faces shocked at what they had just avoided.

Stone explained, "It must have had an altimeter fuse that activated as it descended. I suspect it would have detonated on our approach to landing."

"Anything else you want to tell me about Agent Stone?"

"No, sir, that's it for now," Stone sat back in his chair, buckling himself as the cargo door closed and the cabin repressurized.

Stone sat and reflected on what he had just seen. Someone wanted him out of the way.

CHAPTER 18 (A little white lie)

Jacob and Anya sat in the living room, watching the local channel as Dmitri and his men unloaded the food and alcohol they had just purchased in the village. Cases of vodka and whiskey were stacked on the wine cellar floor. One of the guards placed a 15-year-old bottle of Pappy Van Winkle on the table in front of Anya and Jacob, along with two glasses, and then walked away.

"Oh, very nice. This must be for you to enjoy. I told my uncle it was your favorite." Anya leaned over to the table in front of the couch, opened the bottle of brown liquid, and poured a small amount into the glass. She handed it to Jacob just as the Italian news broadcaster reported a story showing a photo that made Jacob put his glass down. On the screen was an official photograph of Supervising Special Agent Cassius Stone.

"Anya, what is she saying?" Jacob said slowly, concentrating on the screen.

"She is saying that a Military aircraft leaving a base in Germany is missing at sea. The plane had four crew members and a Department of the Treasury Agent. Search efforts are underway to locate the plane; however, it was flying without identifying signals, so its exact location or direction of travel is unknown." Anya sat quietly, looking at Jacob.

"What the hell happened?" Jacob said as he watched the screen. Images of Navy ships and aircraft covering large sections of the ocean were shown. A map displaying a yellow line from Germany to Washington, D.C. was shown, and Jacob could make out the word "Ramstein" from the reporter.

"Your boss appears to have gotten into some bad luck. So, we don't have to worry about him looking for you," Anya said as she took a sip of whiskey.

Jacob sat, shocked by what he saw. Is this what Dmitri meant about his people taking care of things? Did they blow up Stone's aircraft to get him out of the way? Things were getting complicated, Jacob thought to himself, yet they were also becoming very clear.

Jacob thought this was an opportunity. He stood up and left the room, exiting the villa without saying a word. The others watched, and one guard started walking towards the door as if to shadow him. However, Anya spoke out.

"He needs time to process this; let him be," she instructed the man.

The guard stopped and looked at Dmitri for instructions. The older man was preparing some meat and cheese, a knife in one hand, slowly slicing a chunk of meat from the roasted chicken on the kitchen counter. He looked at the guard and shook his head. The guard understood, returning to the chair he had just occupied.

Jacob meandered down the orderly rows of grapevines, each step a deliberate stride through the fertile expanse of the vineyard. Pausing to inhale deeply, he let the crisp air fill his lungs, mingling with the faint scent of earth and the promise of impending rain hinted at by the gathering clouds. Memories stirred within him, transporting him back to a simpler time of childhood innocence, where he lay nestled between his parents on the soft grass, gazing skyward at the whimsical dance of fluffy white clouds drifting in the blue canvas above.

"What do you see, Jacob?" his mother's gentle voice would inquire, punctuating the serene tableau with her tender curiosity.

"A horse, running," he would reply, his imagination sculpting the shape-shifting clouds into fantastical creatures that galloped across the heavens.

Though well-intentioned, his mother's words, "Horses are very strong, like you," offered scant solace in the face of life's trials. Yet they bestowed upon him a fleeting sense of reassurance, a notion that perhaps strength lay dormant within him, waiting to be summoned.

"When you feel unhappy, I want you to think about that horse and how strong you are," his father would add, his voice a comforting presence beside him, even as the shadows of his own affliction loomed on the horizon.

Lost in trance amidst the fragrant embrace of the vineyard, Jacob's internal monologue echoed with newfound resolve. "I need to be the horse. I can get through this," he murmured softly to himself, the weight of solitude pressing heavily upon him. His mother's absence, his father's ailing memory, and his mentor's puzzling absence all converged to cast a shadow over his spirit.

Drawing a steadying breath, Jacob sought refuge in the sanctuary of memory, conjuring the image of Lisa, a beacon of simplicity in a sea of complexity. Recollections of their shared moments in his San Francisco apartment flooded his mind, where the intricacies of their relationship had once seemed the greatest of burdens. Yet, with the clarity of hindsight, he realized that the past held its own brand of ease, its own semblance of simplicity that eluded the tumult of the present.

Contemplating the passage of time, Jacob's thoughts drifted to a distant horizon, where the vineyard stood as a silent witness to the ebb and flow of life. Would he, in five years' time, look back upon this moment with a wistful nostalgia, yearning for the tranquility it afforded amidst life's tempestuous currents? Or would it be but a fleeting memory, obscured by the passage of time and the relentless march of circumstance? Only time would tell, as Jacob stood amidst the whispering vines, a solitary figure amidst the timeless beauty of the Italian countryside.

He removed the Sat phone from his pocket and debated about activating it. Would that send a signal that could show his location? He pressed the activation button while holding down the five key. The screen on the phone came to life, displaying the second telecommunications line was active and waiting. Jacob typed the word "STATUS," hoping Stone would reply with something. Send. Jacob waited, but no message. After five minutes, Jacob turned off the phone, sliding it back into his cargo pants pocket. His stomach felt odd, the same way it felt when Tonya called him years ago to tell him that Lisa was lying on the pavement with a bullet in her head.

Slowly walking back towards the villa, Anya approached him. She hugged him without a word as the couple stood amongst the vines, feeling the cool ocean air blow against them.

"I know he was your friend and boss, but we don't know if he was part of the plan to frame you. It is ok to grieve his loss, but remember to keep an open mind that you are being used," she said with her head against his chest.

Being used, he thought. An interesting choice of words to use. As he stood quietly hugging this woman who moved from friend to lover to stranger in the blink of an eye.

"We need to go pack. Uncle has someone for you to meet. I think this will answer your questions and ease your worries," she took Jacob by the hand, slowly walking back to the villa.

"Pack? Where are we going?"

"Home, Jacob."

Jacob stopped and turned to Anya, still holding her hand.

"Home as in the United States? That's not a wise move. You've seen the reports on the news. I'll be arrested as soon as I step off the plane. Is that the plan? Are you guys giving me up already?" he said as he stepped back from Anya.

She smiled, "No, my love, we are doing as we promised. By this time next week, you will be sitting back at your desk, answering phone calls, and protecting America." She said as she made a fist and shook it in the air.

The Amerigo Vespucci Airport in Florence is a fast-paced, densely populated location with its share of daily international travelers; however, not for Jacob and his party. As he began to become accustomed to it, Jacob and Anya, along with several others, accompanied them to a private gate located just west of the main airport. Passing through several gates, the group parked the two large black SUVs near an Embraer EMB 175 private jet. Personnel tended to their luggage as Anya and Jacob boarded the plane and found a comfortable couch to sit on for a fifteen-plus hour flight to Thunder Bay, Canada, with a quick refuel in Greenland.

Jacob took a short nap as Anya read. Sleeping on a plane was always difficult for him as he could never actually fall into a deep sleep, always in a limbo state between twilight and rest. He opened his eyes, sat still, and watched Anya. She was halfway through an old tattered book that looked as if it had been cherished for many years.

"What are you reading?"

"One of my favorites. It was written by your American novelist, Ernest Hemmingway, For Whom the Bell Tolls. I love the hero, Robert Jordan," her eyes not coming off the page she was reading.

"Wasn't Hemmingway a communist?" recalling an article he had read years ago.

"My grandfather said he was a fighter against the Marxists and Fascists. He sided with the Communists; however, I do not believe he was a member."

"Your grandfather? Did he study Hemingway?"

"They were close friends. My Grandfather gave me this book when I was very young," she opened the book to the front and turned it to Jacob. The signature of Ernest Hemingway was written on the page.

"He signed the book for your grandfather? Wow, that has to be valuable."

"Yes, I would think so. They would meet and drink at the El Floridita Bar in Havana. They had met after a funeral for a friend, Jacob Golos, and Hemingway gave the book to my grandfather as a gift. I always knew him as Mr. Argo. It wasn't until many years later that I learned his true name, Ernest Hemingway. He wrote a lot and had many cats, is what I remember being told."

"I've never read the book but have always wanted to," Jacob said.

"It is a story about loyalty and love. The love story between Robert Jordan and Maria is wonderful. It reminds me of us when we first met," looking up a Jacob and smiling.

"Well, now I have to read it," giving Anya a wink and a smile.

As the plane came to a stop outside the fuel area of Kangerlussuaq Airport, Greenland, several passengers stepped out to stretch their legs and smoke. The sun had just risen, and the landscape was barren. An icecap could be seen in the distance. The air was cold, and Jacob looked around, thinking what a desolate piece of Earth he was occupying. The guards on the plane had changed from their two-piece suits to casual, log-sleeve plaid shirts and black or khaki cargo pants. Jacob found it amusing that the only people who thought they didn't look out of place were the ones who actually did.

Anya stepped up to Jacob, putting her arm through his as she inspected the landscape. They could see their breath in the air. Neither said a word; the only sound was of the gas truck refueling the plane.

"I have not seen any further reports on the aircraft Stone was flying on," Anya said, knowing this was on Jacob's mind.

"Thanks, are you hungry?" Jacob asked.

"No, I'm just tired of flying. I want to fall into a nice bed and reset my body clocks," Anya said as a plane crew member yelled out that they were ready to go. The passengers slowly made their way back to the plane as it taxied, eventually lifting off and rising into the clouds.

Jacob leaned his head back, closing his eyes. This time, sleep came a bit easier. His mind cleared, and thoughts of jail, prosecution, and capture no longer flashed on the screen of his memory. Flashbacks of Lisa came to mind. He thought about their apartment and how it felt with the windows open and the Bay wind blowing through. Then his thoughts took a dark turn. The moment he had been lifted and thrown over the ship's railing, and his slow-motion descent into a cold Pacific Ocean. He began to breathe rapidly and wanted to wake up from the dream until something woke him.

"Ladies and Gentlemen, we are on our approach to the Thunder Bay International Airport. We should be arriving in fifteen minutes." The announcement over the cabin speakers awoke Jacob, who had lain down on the couch and was covered by a blanket. A couple of the guards were finishing a bottle of Jack Daniels, as Anya was finishing up in the lavatory. She had changed into a tight-fitting jumpsuit, which gave her a very militaristic appearance.

Rubbing the sleep from his eyes, Jacob looked out the window as the plane gently landed and maneuvered to a private parking area. Three Cadillac SUVs were waiting, along with their drivers. Jacob could feel his anxiety growing as they prepared to leave. No one from customs had approached them for passports or identification, and this felt strange. Scanning the fence line for occupied cars that might be waiting for the convoy to depart brought nothing suspicious in sight.

"I'm concerned we will have trouble at the border. Have you guys thought about that?" he whispered to Anya.

"Not to worry, my love, we have it all under control," as she reopened her book and continued reading. The driver would occasionally glance in the mirror, looking at Jacob as if still not trusting the new guy. "Back at ya, bro," Jacob thought.

As the convoy slowed and crossed the Pigeon River on the international bridge of Highway 61, Jacob watched for anything unusual. People that might be in the bushes, cars out of place, but there was nothing. His sense of alertness increased as he considered his options. Bailing from the SUV and trying to make cover in the dense woods could be an option, but they were out in the middle of nowhere. Just sit tight and let this play out, he thought.

The officer manning the border station approached the open window of the SUV, looking inside at the passengers. Everyone maintained a stoic look forward, showing no emotion.

"Good afternoon. Passports or Visa, please," as the passengers passed their documents to the driver, then handed them to the officer. A few minutes later, the officer returned and, without a question, handed the documents back and smiled. "Welcome to the United States," he said.

Jacob thought he could hear his heartbeat as they drove into the U.S. He sighed and took a moment to regain his thoughts.

"Idiot," mumbled the man sitting to Jacobs' left.

"I told you, nothing to worry about," Anya said, closing her book.

"So now what, where do we go?" Jacob asked.

"A cute little store down the road. We have a very special person for you to meet. There will be some reporters there who might want to ask you questions. Just tell them you have nothing to say. Like when you won the Anastasia Dream," she smiled.

"Reporters? Why would they be there?"

"You are about to be famous again, Jacob. You are the agent who was betrayed by his country, only to be found innocent. It will all make sense in a couple of minutes."

Time hung heavy like a shroud within the confines of Rydens Border Store, nestled in the heart of Grand Portage, Minnesota, where every ticking second seemed to stretch into eternity as Treasury Agent Jacob Westerly found himself ensnared in a moment of profound disbelief. The atmosphere crackled with an almost palpable tension, suffocating him beneath the weight of impending revelation, threatening to crush the very essence of his being. With each beat of his heart echoing thunderously in his ears, he cast frantic glances in every direction, his senses heightened as he desperately sought any inkling of what tumult was poised to unfurl.

Upon cautiously crossing the threshold into the store's interior, Jacob found himself greeted by a scene awash with the hustle and bustle of journalists converging, their equipment poised like sentinels of the media, ready to capture every fleeting moment. Amidst the orchestrated chaos, he locked eyes with a figure tucked away in the corner, a sight that nearly caused his heart to falter within his chest. It was Assistant Director Jonathan "Jack" Bennett, garbed in the guise of a humble angler, his gaze fixed upon fishing paraphernalia adorning the wall. With a subtle gesture, Bennett beckoned Jacob closer, blending seamlessly into the background, unrecognized by the throng of reporters.

As Jacob tentatively approached, uncertainty gnawed at him, grappling with the appropriate address for the enigmatic figure before him. Should he acknowledge Bennett by name, or was there a more discreet approach warranted in this clandestine encounter?

"I will introduce you," Bennett began, his voice a low murmur amidst the frenetic energy of the room, "I'll tell the reporters of your wrongful accusation, our office's relentless pursuit of truth, and the revelation of Kremlin involvement in the theft of your service weapon and the subsequent demise of their own operative, on that rooftop. You will not entertain questions, is that clear?" With a firm handshake sealing their unspoken accord, Jacob offered a silent nod of acquiescence.

"Are you the Praetorian?" Jacob's inquiry slipped from his lips in a hushed whisper, tinged with an undercurrent of trepidation.

A steely glint flickered in Bennett's gaze as he fixed Jacob with an unwavering stare. His response was a stern admonition cloaked in the shadow of consequences.

"Should that name dare to escape your lips once more, the very fabric of our carefully laid plans will unravel in an instant for you. Do you understand?" Jacob swallowed hard, his compliance affirmed with a solemn nod.

"Excellent. Let's get this party started," Bennett declared with a tone that carried across the room, punctuating the onset of their orchestrated unveiling to the awaiting press.

Bennett stepped up to the microphones with Jacob standing just behind him. The reporters and cameramen, noticing that an old fisherman was at the microphones, stopped and trained their cameras on him.

"Thank you, everyone, for coming today. I'm Assistant Treasury Director Jack Bennett, in charge of the Financial Crimes Unit. I decided at the last minute to hold this gathering, and I would like to apologize for my appearance. However, I'm actually on vacation. After this press conference, I plan to go out and catch some big fish!" Bennett spoke in a jesting voice that grabbed a couple of laughs from the confused reporters.

Suddenly, a figure emerged from the backroom, and Jacob's breath caught in his throat. It was Cassius Stone, standing tall and resolute, defying the grave fate that had seemed to claim him. The relief that washed over Jacob was quickly eclipsed by a newfound terror. If Stone had returned, then who was the true target of the FBI SWAT team's laser sights that were active on Jacob's chest?

As the SWAT team closed in, their rifles trained on Jacob, panic coursed through his veins. The world around him blurred, and time slowed to a crawl. Thoughts of betrayal and impending doom swirled in his mind as he braced himself for the inevitable arrest or volley of bullets, which he believed was destined to mark the end of his life.

But in a breathtaking twist of fate, the laser sights shifted, their piercing beams now directed at the one they had pursued relentlessly—the Praetorian himself, Jack Bennett, a Russian asset disguised as a guardian of justice, standing before them.

The few reporters that Bennet has invited to witness the reinstatement of Westerly as a Federal Agent, along with the explanation of the setup by hostile intelligence agencies, never came. Instead, reporters took cover or ran out the door, seeing the FBI SWAT teams descend on the man with his hands slowly raising above his head as they yelled instructions to him not to move.

The realization crashed over Jacob like a tidal wave, shattering the illusion of his imminent demise. He was not the target; he was an unwitting pawn in a grand scheme orchestrated by Bennett, one of the puppet masters pulling the strings from within the very heart of the agency they had sworn to protect. This was the man who planned it all. He was the one who tried to have the two of them killed.

In that climactic moment, Jacob Westerly realized that his journey had only just begun. The shadows of betrayal and the echoes of his near-death experience would forever mold him, forging a resolve that could not be extinguished.

As the SWAT team subdued the fallen Praetorian, Jacob found solace in the knowledge that redemption and justice were within reach. Stone walked over to him and Jacob could not help but reach out, giving Stone a hug, his arms at his side.

"You know Westerly, you're a very touchy-feely kind of guy," Stone's head slightly cocked to the side with a smirk on his face.

"Just glad you didn't crash that plane, they're very expensive," giving Stone a smile.

"If you hadn't given me that name Cerberus, I would have never unlocked the photos and seen the same box that was sitting in front of me on the plane—the one with a fairly large bomb in it."

The SWAT team led Bennett past both agents, handcuffed and looking a bit angry. Not a word was said. Jacob quickly turned as they walked Bennett out the door.

"Anya! She was outside," Jacob said as he followed quickly to the door.

Outside, Anya, Dimitri, and the private guards were handcuffed, standing face against the store wall as officers searched each one, removing weapons and personal belongings. Anya was moved to a seat in a black van, the same kind Jacob recalled seeing her in years ago when they stood at the docks in front of his boat. This time he prayed she would be in an orange jumpsuit much longer than the last time she wore it. He made his way over to the van, where an FBI Agent slid the door open, allowing Jacob a moment with the handcuffed woman.

"Jacob…" she began to say but was interrupted.

"No, Anya, not this time."

"You cannot trust them, Jacob. You saw what they were going to do with you until we stepped in. You watched it on the news, remember?"

"The Italian news report, the one at exactly 4 p.m. Thanks to our colleagues at Italian Interpol and one of their female agents, who had a little broadcast experience, that report said exactly what we wanted it to say. I knew they would show it at 4 p.m., and that's why I had you turn on the TV. The cop you shot, well, I'm sure it was reported, and soon your photo will be on the news as the shooter!"

"I don't believe you. I heard you talking with Stone."

"At 4:45 p.m., just as planned. When the files on the camera card were examined, we learned everything. Fortunately, Nabil was a little too complete, taking photos of emails and schedules of Dark Fleet ships. When we saw Bennett's name on the list and his DNA on the Mussolini letter, everything changed. Our orders came from the White House. Just like you told me years ago, Anya, how does it feel to be a pawn in a much larger game?"

She turned and smiled at Jacob, gently rubbing both hands on her stomach. "Great! Daddy." The door slid shut, and the van pulled away, as she continued to stare at Jacob.

Jacob, stunned at what he had just heard, stepped back, staring at the departing van as it drove off, heading to a Federal holding center in Minneapolis. Sitting on the wooden bench in front of the store gave Jacob a feeling of safety. The world was moving around him. Reporters paid no attention to him as they had just interviewed Stone extensively. Noticing he was sitting alone, Stone walked over and sat next to Jacob.

Stone turned on his tablet and tuned to MSNBC, which had live feeds from news affiliates around the world, reporting on dozens of people under arrest as spies. A scene at Dimitris' villa, where the high-end cars and artifacts stolen by Anya and Peter's cabal were being loaded onto car transporter trucks as law enforcement walked about, taking inventory.

"As I told you on your first day, it really pisses me off when people take things from me. By the way, what did Anya say in the van?" Stone asked.

"I'm a daddy," without emotion on his face.

CHAPTER 19 (Pardon me)

San Francisco was still foggy and still under construction. Jacob looked out the window of his Waymo self-driving Jaguar as it navigated through traffic. He couldn't help but keep his attention on the steering wheel of the empty seat. The years spent in the tech world prepared him for driverless vehicles, artificial intelligence, and all the innovations that had come rushing forward in the past decade.

His cell phone alerted him to an incoming email. Jacobs' training placed him in the peculiar position of never ignoring what could be either a new assignment or a lead from anyone, including the CIA or Israel's 8200 unit. This high-tech Israeli intelligence corps provided him with intel while he navigated through Seoul. The unit could access any computer or cell phone remotely, track them, or even listen to conversations or read text in real time. However, when he opened the email, he stared at the screen in disbelief. The Waymo computer voice informed Jacob that he had arrived at his destination; however, Jacob's hearing was muted in shock.

To: Special Agent Jacob Westerly,

Subject: Termination – Jacob Westerly

Pursuant to President Trump's Executive Order to reduce waste and inefficiency, your services at the Treasury Department are no longer required, effective immediately. Please return all government property, including your badge, laptop, duty weapon, and access credentials. Security will assist with the offboarding process. I appreciate your contributions, but this role is no longer a suitable fit. I wish you the best of luck in your future endeavors.

– Elon Musk, Department of Government Efficiency (DOGE)

Jacob got out of the car, nearly stepping in front of a passing car that brought him out of a momentary daze. He looked off into the distance, feeling numb and confused. As he gained his wits, he pushed the number 1 on his phone, which had Cassius Stone's phone number on quick dial.

"Jacob, I take it you got the email?" Stone inquisitively.

"You knew about this?"

"We've all known the hammer could fall. Did you think you were immune or something?"

"No, I guess not, but, huh, I just figured it was everyone else, not us. We're doing an important job, why reduce our forces?"

"We're doing an important job? Unlike the scientists who research cancer, or the air traffic controllers ensuring we don't have accidents at thirty thousand feet. Or maybe the school teachers who educate our kids, or the park employees who keep rat shit off the ground so our families don't get sick. Everyone has a job that affects someone else; you just don't see them. But now, we're all on the chopping block,"

"Including you?" Jacob asked softly.

"Including me. I have no idea if I'll be gone tonight, tomorrow, or next month. But that's not the half of it. Remember when the President handed out pardons like monopoly money? Well, his other list came out an hour ago."

"Anyone we know?" Jacob asked.

"Yeah, two. Your ex-wife and my ex-boss. Guess the man in the corner office didn't want any of his best friends' associates to be in orange jumpsuits,"

Jacob dropped his phone and leaned against the building. Fired, his criminal homicidal wife, free and the mastermind of it all, out. Jacob felt as though the wind had been sucked from his lungs.

What next, he thought.

ACKNOWLEDGMENTS

The author wishes to acknowledge the invaluable assistance of the following people:

Catherine Schloss
Steven Schloss
Richard Schloss
David Taylor, Head of Curriculum, Lloyd's Maritime Academy
Lt. Col. Tosh "Visa" Smith, USAF (Ret.)
Ede Voorheis, PA
Mike and Sam Boomer, Ryden's Border Store, Minnesota

If you enjoyed this book, please leave a review at the
book store or online retailer where you made your purchase.

You can also leave reviews on Amazon.com, even
if you did not purchase it there. Thanks

To learn how it all started, check out Sanction 23, the first book in the Jacob Westerly series.

Lockheed Martin C130J Super Hercules

Learn more about the C-130 J
Source: File: C-130 J   *Click here for more information.*
          https://en.wikipedia.org/wiki/Lockheed_Martin_C-130J_Super_Hercules

Photo by Jetijones

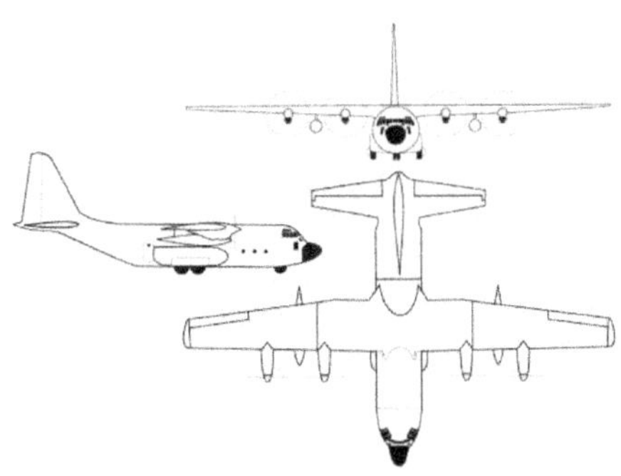